A Jones

Poems and Songs

Written in Spare Moments

A Jones

Poems and Songs
Written in Spare Moments

ISBN/EAN: 9783337179335

Printed in Europe, USA, Canada, Australia, Japan

Cover: Foto ©Andreas Hilbeck / pixelio.de

More available books at **www.hansebooks.com**

Poems and Songs.

WRITTEN IN SPARE MOMENTS

BY

MRS. A. JONES,

ASHTON-ON-RIBBLE.

THERE are many precious moments too often thrown away,
Which, if we would improve them, we should find another day :
We do not know the future, nor what we may require,
But for what we have the talent we always may aspire.
These few and simple verses, in spare moments have been penn'd,
And that any one who reads them will their kind indulgence lend,
    Is the earnest hope of THE AUTHOR.

SECOND EDITION.

PRICE 1 6; POST FREE 1 9.

COPIES MAY BE HAD FROM—

THE AUTHOR, A. JONES, ASHTON-ON-RIBBLE;
MR. BEATTIE, PHOTOGRAPHER, FISHERGATE, NEAR THE STATION, PRESTON ;
MR. WORTHINGTON, STATIONER, FYLDE ROAD, PRESTON.

COPYRIGHT.

Communication received by the Authoress.

BUCKINGHAM PALACE,

May 27th, 1890.

General Sir H. Ponsonby is commanded by the QUEEN to thank Mrs. Jones for her letter of the 23rd inst., and for the copy of her Poems.

EXTRACTS FROM OTHER LETTERS.

From Sir Evan Morris, Mayor of Wrexham.

THE PRIORY, WREXHAM,

14th June, 1889

Dear Madam,

I am obliged by your letter and appropriate verses on Her Majesty's visit to Wales, and with your permission, will have them published.

I am, yours truly,

EVAN MORRIS.

Mrs. A. Jones,
Ash Grove, Ashton-on-Ribble.

ST JOHNS COLLEGE, GRIMSARGH,

12th July, 1888.

Dear Mrs. Jones,

Your poems are unique, simple, and beautiful.

T. ABBOTT PETERS, M.A., Principal

CALDER MOUNT, GARSTANG.

Dear Madam,

I am pleased with the kindly and Christian spirit which pervades your book.

Yours sincerely,

CHARLES WILSON

BROOKLANDS, ASHTON-ON RIBBLE.

12 11/89.

Dear Mrs. Jones,

In my opinion your verses possess considerable artistic merit, in proof of which I send you a written order for twenty copies if you conclude to have them printed and published.

Believe me, yours truly,

W. CALDERWOOD.

We have received a copy of a volume of poems and songs (Preston, R. Parkinson and Co.), by Mrs. A Jones, of Ashton-on-Ribble. The book is dedicated to Lord Winmarleigh, and the Queen has just accepted a copy of the work. Some of the poems would do credit to an author of considerable pretensions. A great variety of subjects are dealt with—many of them of local interest—and the author has sought to give simple and direct expression to her thoughts. Her work is free from any affectations or extravagances of style. At times her muse halts a little, but her love of nature is genuine, and the sentiments she expresses—often with much felicity—are simple and sincere.

DEDICATED

BY PERMISSION

ence

TO

LORD WINMARLEIGH

BY

THE AUTHOR.

PREFACE.

It is with considerable diffidence I lay my little volume of Poems and Songs before a discriminating public, but with the hope that they may be appreciated by many, who, like myself, have not had the advantage of a literary education. I am fully conscious they have grammatical defects; but they are the production, the simple and natural thoughts of one born and reared amid the rural scenes I have attempted to describe, and which I found a source of extreme gratification to occupy my spare moments, which was my only object when I commenced writing them. On the advice and encouragement of my friends, from whom I have received many flattering acknowledgments, I send them forth to the world, with the hope that they may meet with a favourable reception from the very numerous class of readers to which I belong, and who prefer simplicity to those of higher merit. Hoping they may find a response in the hearts of many who are loyal to their Queen and country, also those who admire nature in all her various phases, and give the reader the same amount of enjoyment they have done the writer.

A. JONES.

Ash Grove,
 Ashton-on-Ribble, February 1st. 1890.

CONTENTS.

CONTENTS.—*Continued*

CONTENTS.—*Continued.*

THE HEIR OF WINMARLEIGH.

GLAD was the day, Winmarleigh's heir,
    His grandsire's hope and pride,
Became of age, rejoicings were
    Kept up on every side.
Friends and tenants, servants too,
    All met to wish him joy ;
The aged lord looked on with pride,
    And blessed his noble boy.

With costly gifts friends came from far,
    And kindest wishes poured
Upon the youthful soldier's head,—
    Winmarleigh's future lord ;
And banners waved on tower and hall,
    O'er that gay festive scene :
To many on those broad domains,
    It seemed a fairy dream.

The tables groaned beneath the weight
    Of viands rich and rare ;
The noblest of fair England's sons,
    And daughters, too, were there.
And many tillers of the soil,
    With honest heart and hand,
Whose locks had grown a silvery white,
    On brave Winmarleigh's land.

The son and sire, sat side by side,
　Around the festal board ;
And every bold yeoman there,
　Was glad to call them lord.
The noble matron on their right,
　Looked on her soldier son ;
And thank'd kind heaven for sending her
　That loved and only one.

With happy hearts, they all enjoyed,
　That banqnet and fair scene ;
And toasts were drunk right royally,
　To country, and their Queen.
Commerce, and agriculture, too,
　In that baronial hall,
Were toasted : and at night they all
　Enjoyed a splendid ball.

Sweet strains of music echoed through
　Those chambers long and wide ;
And all went merry, as if for
　A young and happy bride.
The scion of that grand old home,—
　Last of his noble race,
With gracious words and genial smiles,
　Right well adorned his place.

And for the children of the schools,
　A sumptuous feast was spread ;
And with their cheers the welkin rang,
　Ere they went home to bed.
Old Punch and Judy, too, were there,
　To entertain the young ;
And lantern, with its magic slides,
　Made merry all the throng.

And of fireworks in the evening,—
  So grand was the display,
That neither old or young will e'er,
  Forget that gala day.
The aged lord with silvery locks,
  Was happiest of the band ;
He moved among his noble guests :
  A very king so grand.

    *   •   •   •   •

A year has passed : a mournful gloom
  Hangs o'er Winmarleigh now ;
That cherished darling helpless lies,
  The death damps on his brow.
With tend'rest care his mother soothes
  His sufferings day and night ;
But e'en a mother's love could not
  Put that dread foe to flight.

The youthful heir was doomed to leave
  His heritage so grand ;
The mournful tidings sent a thrill
  Of gloom throughout the land.
All hearts went out on that sad day
  Unto the aged lord ;
When lifeless they brought home his son :
  He looked, but spoke no word.

His prop, his pride, his hope was gone :
  He bravely bore the blow ;
And meekly bow'd to the decree
  Of Him who will'd it so.
In state they laid him in the room,
  That one short year before,
Echoed with festive joy and mirth :
  The gayest he was there.

They bore him gently to the tomb,
  For ever there to rest ;
His helmet and his sword were laid,
  Useless across his breast.
Had he been spared he might have won.
  His grandsire's honoured fame ;
But now, alas ! he's gone ! the last
  Of that illustrious name.

Bright floral wreaths of every hue,
  Were sent from far and near,
To grace that fair youth's burial :
  Beloved by all so dear.
Alas ! alas ! for human hopes,
  How frail to lean upon ;
Exultingly we see them near,
  We grasp them : they are gone i

He'd gained the love of high and low,
  If spared to them he'd been ;
His loyal purpose was to serve
  His country and his Queen.
But in the morning of his life,
  His bright young spirit fled ;
The youthful heir of Winmarleigh,
  Was numbered with the dead !

Mysterious are the ways of Him,
  Who doeth all things well ;
We may not question His designs,
  His wisdom or His skill.
But in submission meekly bow,
  And trust His saving grace ;
No cross to bear, no crown to wear,
  When we shall see His face.

ON THE BIRTHDAY OF HER MAJESTY QUEEN VICTORIA.

YEAR OF JUBILEE.

AGAIN with joy and gladness, the natal day appears,
Of our gracious sovereign lady who has ruled us fifty years ;
Each one has added greatness to our country and our Queen,
Long may she live to bless us, in our hearts she reigns supreme.

The bells ring out their joyous peals, on this her natal morn,
Earth was clothed in richest beauty, when our gracious Queen
       was born ;
In the gladness of the Maytime began her noble life,—
Her every thought's been duty, as Maiden, Queen, and Wife.

On castle, hall, and tower, banners float upon the breeze ;
And her loyal sable armies, far away across the seas,
Assemble in their forces to display their strength and might,—
Ready, eager, able, to put all her foes to flight.

Although a mighty monarch, to her subjects she's a friend ;
Her tenderness and sympathy is noble, great, and grand ;
She moves among her people with dignity and grace,
And with perfect adoration they look upon her face.

Millions will bless and greet her with loyal hearts to-day,—
All nations' tongues and people for her safety ever pray ;
To the humblest of her subjects she lends a list'ning ear,
And will strive to heal their sorrows, and wipe their bitter tear.

She is great in her dominions, her glory and her power,
But a little child might lead her to the suffering and the poor ;
How many eyes grow brighter with the thought that England's
       Queen,
To make their burdens lighter, 'neath their humble roof had
       been.

God bless our Queen and country ! and may each passing year,
With honour, peace, and plenty, our hearts and homes still cheer
God bless the olive branches ! that round about her shine,
With length of days and happiness, with peace and love divine.

A SONG OF WELCOME TO QUEEN VICTORIA,

On Her visit to Wales. August 24, 1889.

Arise, arise, lift up your hearts and voices,
   Ye sons of Cambria let the echoes ring ;
Unfurl your banners on your towers and mountains,
   Give to your Queen a royal welcoming.

Chorus—

   Shout, shout, till all the mountains echo,
   Your songs of welcome to our gracious Queen.

Ye joyous bells ring out your peals of gladness,
   In loyal welcome to our Queen to day ;
Ring, ring, triumphant peals for India's Empress,
   Whose sable millions homage to her pay.

She comes to Wales, not conquering, or to conquer :
   Peace and good-will reign in her heart supreme ;
Minstrels, come tune your harps, and swell the chorus
   In joyful welcome to our gracious Queen.

Long hath she reigned, and long may she reign o'er us :
   Plenty and peace still flourish in our vales.
God bless and save our gracious Queen Victoria ;
   And bless her noble son, our Prince of Wales.

ODE TO THE PRIMROSE.

IN MEMORIAM TO THE LATE EARL BEACONSFIELD, WHO DIED APRIL 19, 1881.

BEAUTIFUL primrose ! whose home is the bowers,
Where the nightingale sings to thy odorous flowers ;
Alone in thy beauty like stars in the sky,
Thou bringest glad tidings that spring time is nigh.

By rippling streamlets, in forest and dell,
Where all is sweet peace thou delightest to dwell ;
Where the thrush o'er thy soft couch pours forth his lay,
And awakes thee from slumber at dawning of day.

Beautiful primrose ! how welcome thy flowers,
When thou returnest with spring's balmy hours ;
Lowly and simple thy pale starry blooms,
But welcome and prized in the proudest of homes.

Many will wear thy sweet blossoms to-day,
In memory of him who hath long passed away :
A sweet silent tribute to England's great Earl,
No need for her people their flags to unfurl.

Beautiful primrose ! the great ones now roam
To seek for thy blooms in thy fair woodland home ;
Thy patron hath made thee a name in the land,
Great as the rose, or the broom* can command.

When they bore him at last to his eternal rest,
A wreath of thy blossoms was laid on his breast ;
Fresh with the dewdrops, and gentle spring showers,
Loving hands placed on his bier thy flowers.

* Plantagenet.

Thou art brought from thy humble but soft mossy bed,
As a tribute of love to the mighty one dead ;
Queens and princesses scorn not thy birth,
Thou wert the beloved of the noblest on earth.

He went to his rest when thy blooms were so bright,
With the genial day, and the dew-drops at night ;
And garlands we'll weave of them now to his name,
And lift up our voices in songs of his fame.

Thy lovely pale blossoms were much more to him,
Than simply a flower by the river's cool brim ;
He felt that to raise up our thoughts thou wert given,
And make us more fit for a bright home in heaven.

Then hail to thee, primrose ! and hail to the bowers !
Where nature once placed thee, the humblest of flowers ;
But to their great leagues† they now give thy fair name,
O'er which none may preside, but squire or dame.

The page‡ that records their deeds too, bears thy name :
How the rose and the lily must envy thy fame ;
Thou art sought for and placed on royalties' breast,
On the day England mourns for her noblest and best.

A LAMENT FOR THE RIVER RIBBLE.

Oh ! what has become of our beautiful river,
   Ebbing and flowing its high banks between ?
Gone are its beauties, departed for ever,—
   Desolate and drear is the once charming scene.

† Primrose League.   ‡ Primrose Chronicle.

We loved the fair stream, and were proud of its beauty :
    The healthful sea-breezes that came with the tide
Imparted new life ; and we thought it a duty
    To bring there our sick ones to rest by its side.

A calm and sweet peace o'er our senses came stealing,
    As we sat on its banks 'mid pastoral scenes ;
And the sweet chimes o'er the water came pealing,—
    Mingling their tones with the flow of the streams.

In fine summer evenings, great was the pleasure
    To walk on its banks, or row o'er its tide ;
Our river to us was a blessing and treasure :
    We bewail its sad loss, let who may deride.

And the trim little vessels rode by so lightly,
    With white sails outspread, like a bird on the wing ;
The jack-tars who mann'd them, looking so sprightly,
    And captains important as if they were king.

Alas ! for the day we heeded the tempter,
    Who told us that riches would roll up its streams,
If they might make it for big ships to enter :
    But now we are woke from our illusive dreams.

Oh ! what a scene of sad chaos now meets us :
    We gaze with dismay on the rubbish piled high ;
The sea-gulls, like vultures, all screaming to greet us :
    Well may we linger,—afraid to go nigh.

But stay ; there's a band of heroes united,
    And pledged to redeem a great part of our loss,
Hurrah for their courage ! they deserve to be knighted,
    If they can clear up this deplorable mess.

BOATING ON THE DEE, IN THE MONTH OF JUNE.

On the winding Dee we're gliding so lightly,
    Through the green meadows where golden cups gleam ;
Our fairy boat rides o'er the water so sprightly,
    Past the white lilies that float on the stream.

High over our heads the lark sings so sweetly,
    And the shy cuckoo is piping his lay ;
Over the river the swallows dart fleetly,
    Where gnats gyrate in the summer's bright ray.

Roses and eglantine crown the thick bushes,
    Their odorous perfume floats on the soft air ;
They scatter their treasures among the tall rushes,
    That shelter the home, the heron finds there.

Onward we glide 'neath the willow's long tresses,
    And whispering alders that hang o'er its tides ;
Where tall ferns abound, and the greenest of cresses,
    In richness and beauty embellish its sides.

And stately foxgloves above them are bending,
    Their bright purple bells the steep slopes adorn ;
And crystal streams from the mountain descending,
    Add to the scene a most beautiful charm.

The stock-doves above, their love-notes are cooing,
    In the old oaks that for ages have stood ;
And the sleek herds on the emerald banks lowing,
    Or up to their knees in the river's cool flood.

Not the Rhine with its vines, its rocks, and its castles,
    Can vie with the beautiful vales of the Dee ;
The homes on its banks, that peacefully nestles,
    Hath delighted the heart of a monarch to see.

THE SANCTITY OF MARRIAGE.

WRITTEN IN ANSWER TO MRS. MONA CARD, SUGGESTING THE DISSOLUTION OF UNHAPPY MARRIAGES.

Mrs. Mona lacks experience or she would never try,
To influence her sisters to break the marriage tie ;
We should soon be like the Mormons, and that would never do,
Every thoughtful woman, the proposal would pooh-pooh.

On the day we were married, we pledged ourselves for life,
To be unto our husband a faithful loving wife ;
And if he fail in duty, are we to fail in ours ?
No, never, Mrs. Mona, however dark the hours.

We know the day was happiest we ever spent in life,
When at the church's altar we were made a wedded wife ;
And shall we break the vows that we plighted on that day,
Because, forsooth, we cannot just always have our way.

The marriage tie is binding, and never must be broke,
Tho' the fetters become galling, we still must bear the yoke ;
To leave our home and children would be a wicked sin,
For soon another woman would be sure to enter in.

Shall we be like a garment they've wore till they are tired,
Or like a piece of furniture, sometime they may have hired ;
Of which they've grown quite weary, and long for something
    new :
No, thank you, Mrs. Mona, I don't agree with you.

How the men would be delighted with Mrs. Mona's plan :
They would only have a shindy to kick up now and then ;
And make us all so weary, and tired of our life,
That in a fit of anger, we'd consent to end the strife.

Oh no, we must never put temptation in their way,
Or give them an excuse for their minds to go astray ;
They may vent their angry passions, or Mrs. Mona preach,
Till death, I'll hold my husband as firmly as a leech.

THERE ARE MOMENTS.

THERE are moments in our lives, when all seems so dark and drear,
As if some impending sorrow to our hearts was drawing near ;
When of life we feel so weary, and so oppressed with care,
That a feeling overwhelms us akin to deep despair ;
When our fondest hopes are blighted, and the world to us appears
A desert or a wilderness, or bitter vale of tears.

And there are happy moments, full of visions fair and bright,
When our hearts are full of gladness, and bounding with delight ;
When all the world is beautiful, our home the sweetest spot,
And our sad and gloomy fancies are for a while forgot ;
We mingle with the joyous throng, who laugh and dance and sing,
And think not what the morrow to their thoughtless hearts may
        bring.

And there are peaceful moments, that calmly glide away,
When we feel a sweet contentment that is neither grave nor gay,
But of both a happy mingling ; together they combine
To make our lives so cheerful we cease then to repine ;
And if we would endeavour to make our lives complete,
We must take without repining, the bitter with the sweet.

And there are, too, spare moments, too often thrown away,
Which if we would improve them, we should find another day ;
We do not know the future, nor what we may require,
But for what we have the talent, we always may aspire ;
So let us improve spare moments, as rapidly they fly :
We never can re-call them, when once they have gone by.

THE BEAUTY OF EARTH.

How beautiful is earth if we look around and see,
Nature her charms displaying wherever we may be ;
There's beauty in the meadows when the grass is springing green,
In the skylark warbling o'er it, in the morning's dewy gleam.

There's beauty in the brooklet that ripples in the dell,
In the bright and shining river, and the music of its swell ;
In the flowers, ferns, and lichens, that flourish by its side,
And the velvet rushes lifting their heads above its tide.

There's beauty in the morning, when all is calm and still,
When the sun in golden glory is rising o'er the hill ;
In the dew-drops that are gleaming on every flower and leaf,
And in the yellow cornfield, when they bind the harvest sheaf.

And when the sun is shining above our heads at noon,
And the wild birds are singing their gayest sweetest tune ;
How sweet it is to wander, or rest in the leafy glade,
And enjoy the quiet beauty 'neath the whispering alder's shade.

And in the calm still evening, when the sun sinks in the west,
A glowing beauty lingers o'er the earth, of peace and rest ;
When the dewy mists are rising above the meadow grass,
And the corn-crake hoarsely greets you in the gloaming as you pass.

And hedges, when the blossoms of the wood-bine round them twine,
Or when the naked branches with crystal frostwork shine ;
All, all are bright and beautiful, and free to every one,
To partake of at their leisure, when their daily labour's done.

The woodlands too are beautiful, with all their varied green,
When primroses are blooming on mossy banks between ;
The tiny linnet singing upon the hawthorn spray,
Rejoicing in the beauty of a bright warm summer day.

In winter when the holly with its scarlet berries gleam,
From out their snowy covering, above the frost-bound stream ;
Gay youths and maidens gliding, in happy careless glee,
Their skates and voices ringing on the air so merrily.

And when the little robin comes on the window sill,
Singing gaily for his crumbs, tho' he feels the winter's chill :
Each picture is so beautiful, I love them all to see
And both summer days and winter are glorious to me.

HAPPY HOMES.

How bright is the morning when o'er the blue mountains
　Bright sunbeams appear and illumine the earth ;
But more bright is the home where love's hallowed fountains,
　Spring in each bosom, and brighten the hearth.

Sweet are the chimes of the distant bells ringing,
　As their tones rise and fall on the soft summer air ;
But sweeter the voices of children when singing,
　As they gather in love round their parent's arm chair.

How healthful and pure are the breezes of morning,
　That sweep o'er the meadow, the mountain, and moor ;
But more pure is the home where love's flame is burning,
　Sweet is its influence, and holy its power.

The house is not home where love is a stranger,
　And each sullen face is o'erclouded with gloom ;
Like the ox to his stall, or the ass to his manger :
　They go there to eat, to sleep, and to groom.

But when loving kindness reigns in each bosom,
　And cheerfulness glows round the bright hearth and board ;
Each face like a rose, in beauty will blossom,
　And a home bright and happy will be their reward.

THE CROAKER.

WRITTEN TO " THE FACTORY TIMES," IN ANSWER TO A
GRUMBLING CORRESPONDENT.

SOME people delight in croaking,—
    And such is the one I may say,
Who sent you those grumbling verses
    That you published the other day.
He speaks of the loom and the spindle
    As if they were objects of dread ;
Instead of the useful inventions
    That provide us with clothes and bread.

Sin and want accompany not labour,—
    It is idleness clothes us in rags,
And prompts us to envy the neighbour
    Who rides in his coaches and gigs.
'Tis when loom and spindle are silent
    That children cry out for bread ;
And the mother is so pained to hear them—
    For food she sells their warm bed.

Talk not of sinning and sorrow,
    Because we've to work for our crust :
It is better to work than to borrow,
    And better to wear than to rust.
Why speak of the factory workers
    As a down-trodden spiritless band ?
They're the very backbone of our nation,—
    The strength and pride of our land ;

Whose genius invented our engines,
    And most of our splendid machines :
Instead of idly complaining,
    They realized wonderful dreams.

And if they love the bright flowers
  That gladden our beautiful earth,
There's a time allotted for all things,—
  Work, recreation, and mirth.

They have plenty of time in the summer,
  When closed for the day are the mills,
To roam about in the meadows,
  Or climb up the air-bracing hills.
When the heat of the day is all over,
  And nightingale warbling his lay :
The enjoyment then is far greater
  Than if they had idled all day.

They may have their trials and troubles, —
  So have all of us while we are here ;
But in mills are both men and women
  Who are happy and live on good cheer.
Whose homes are a picture of neatness,
  Cheerfulness, plenty, and love ;
Who go to church on a Sunday,
  And worship their Father above.

ODE TO THE THRUSH.

PRETTY bird, thy song so sweet,
Each glad morn thou dost repeat.
In the early dawning hours,
When the dew-drops gem the flowers,—
Comes sweet melody divine
From that little throat of thine.
Sweetest minstrel of the grove.

Warbling forth thy happy love,
To thy mate in cosy nest :
Deep affection in thy breast,
For her and her little brood,
Anxious to provide them food.
And when twilight draweth nigh,
Sings thy sweetest lullaby,—
Which to me is sweeter still
Than lark's song, or gushing trill
Of philomel in moonlit bowers,
When his evening song he pours.
Morning, noon, and dewy eve,
Thy song will oft my heart relieve,
From sad thoughts so apt to rise,
And raise my spirits to the skies.

The plough-bo lingers on his way
To listen to thy merry lay,
So sweet and clear, so loud and long,
And tries to imitate the song
That issues from thy tiny throat,
And on the odorous breezes float.
Thy sparkling eye and head aside,
As if thy heart swell'd with glad pride,
For the gift bestowed on thee,
Tho' thou art so wild and free.

What such pleasure e'er can yield,
As to roam in verdant field ?
Rest beneath a blooming thorn—
Its fragrance on the breezes borne ?
List to music such as thine,
Warbled forth in strains so fine ?
Pale primroses blooming round,
Violets nestling on the ground ;

Blue-bells waving in the breeze,
'Neath the shade of forest trees,—
Tinted like the summer skies
In the richest azure dyes ;
Rippling brooklets murmuring near,
Bright as crystal, sweet and clear ?
In such scenes thou bonny bird,
Oft thy glorious voice I've heard,
Till the echoes woke around
In the stillness so profound.
As I listened to thy lays,
My heart o'erflowed in silent praise
To the Maker who hath given,   •
Gifts that raise our hearts to heaven.

GREETINGS TO Mrs. GLADSTONE IN ITALY, DECEMBER 24TH, 1888.

Accept these greetings, noble lady,
    Tho' you are so far away ;
In the hearts and homes of England
    You will live on Christmas day.
To us all a bright example,
    Noble lady, you have been ;
In devotion to your husband,
    To your country, home, and Queen.

And accept congratulations
    On your husband's natal day :
Yours has been the joy to cheer him,
    On his great and glorious way.

Bright your lamp is ever burning,
 Ready for your country's call ;
And when difficulties meet you,
 You press on and face them all.

Eight and fifty years he's serv'd us
 With his great and wondrous mind ;
When shall we another leader
 Equal to him ever find ?
Side by side you've journeyed onward,
 Always girded heart and hand ;
Ready for the call of duty
 In your cause so great and grand

Well you've earned your golden guerdon,—
 Fifty years you've been a crown
To your husband : and your children
 Must be proud of your renown.
They will rise and call you blessed ;
 Long may you yet live to see
Children's children gather round you,
 And a blessing to you be.

May you see your hopes accomplished,
 For the good of Erin's Isle ;
And your noble efforts free her,
 From the stain of so much guile.
Four score years, and yet we find him
 Eager, earnest, vigorous too ;
Thought by many who surround him,
 That he owes it most to you.

How he sways the hearts of thousands,—
 How they hang upon his words ;
Wond'ring at his voice and accent,—
 Sweeter than the song of birds.

'Neath Italian skies of splendour,
   Breathing the delicious air ;
By its lakes and scenes of grandeur,
   May you rest from every care.

And return unto St. Stephen's,
   Hearts and minds still firm and true
To the thistle, rose, and shamrock,
   Aye, and leek of Cambria too.
See the grand old statesman standing
   In the sacred house of prayer ;
Reading words of consolation
   Unto all assembled there.

Nothing feeble in his accents :
   Ringing sweet, and clear, and bold ;
Gifted with a flow of language,
   Like the fishermen of old.
Like a glorious golden sunset,
   Is the evening of his days :
Cheering, blessing, all around him,
   With his bright and kindly ways.

Pardon my presumption, lady,
   In assuming thus to write :
But in kindest, best of wishes,
   Thousands will to day unite.
Tho' my greetings may be humble,
   They are none the less sincere :
And permit me now to wish you, —
   When it comes, — a glad new year.

OH! LET US BE HAPPY.

PRIZE POEM, "PRESTON HERALD," JULY 28th, 188—

Oh let us be happy and cheerful,
   Let us be merry and glad ;
The world will keep moving onward,
   Tho' we should be ever so sad.
If we should meet with misfortune,
   Why need we give way to despair ?
Let "onward" be ever our motto,
   And our aim to drive away care.

What if disappointments come to us,
   Why need we murmur at that ?
When there are so many rich blessings,
   That are sent to brighten our lot.
You ask what those blessings consist of,—
   Wait, friend, and lend me your ear :
They are not to be found in a carriage,
   Nor yet in five thousand a year.

But in always being contented,
   And living a virtuous life ;
In a home we know we can pay for,
   With a nice little good tempered wife.
If in the day we've to labour,
   There is always the night we can rest ;
But if we sit down and be idle,
   We shall soon be corroded with rust.

When friends we have trusted betray us —
   The brother we've lov'd prove unkind ;
Let us strive against all bitter feeling,
   And not let it trouble our mind.

And should we meet with another,
Faint with the heat of the day,
Remember that he is our brother,
And give him a lift on the way.

This life is a long toilsome journey,
We each have our burdens to bear ;
But if all were equally divided,
We might have a much larger share.
Then let us each take up our burden,
And make the best of it we can ;
If at any time it should be heavy,
Let us shoulder it like a true man.'

THE BLIND GIRL TO HER MOTHER.

MOTHER, dear mother, how bright is the day,
Come out and sit where the soft breezes play ;
Sweet and refreshing they waft o'er my brow,
I hear their soft whispers in every bough.
They bear on their wings the perfume of flowers,
And wild bees are humming about in the bowers ;
I hear the birds singing in joyous delight,
They feel that the day is so glorious and bright.

Altho' I'm denied the blessings of sight,
My spirit oft feels so radient and bright ;
I fancy the plumage of beautiful birds
So gorgeous, I cannot describe them in words.
The beautiful flowers that shed their perfume,
I paint in the gayest and brightest their bloom :
Perhaps if I saw them they might not be
So pleasing as they now appear unto me.

I cannot see nature but her glorious voice,
Makes my heart glad and my spirit rejoice ;
The songs of the birds and the wind as it plays,
Sweet as Eolian's melodious lays ;
And its weird moaning to me hath a charm,
When in my bed I am laid snug and warm
And the murmuring streams as they gently glide,
I love to roam near them with you by my side ;
And all to me are so good and so kind,
I am apt to forget, dear mother, I am blind.

LINES ON THE DEATH OF A YOUNG FRIEND, AGED 22.

SHE has gone to her rest, now her troubles are o'er,
And landed, we hope, on Canaan's bright shore ;
No more will she weary with hard toil and care,
Which was more than her strength or spirit could bear.

In silence she suffered, and seldom complained ;
Her young life was blighted, it only remained
For death to approach : in whate'er form he came,
She was ready and waiting, nor questioned his claim.

She has passed away to her rest now on high,
Where neither sickness nor pain can come nigh ;
To a land more congenial, to visions more bright,
Her spirit hath taken its aerial flight.

Like a pale tender lily exposed to the storm,
With the cold blast, of her strength she was shorn ;
Now her spirit hath cast off its tenement of clay,
And soar'd in its lightness to eternal day.

THE SILVER WEDDING.

WRITTEN OCTOBER 11, 1884. THE FIRST SOD CUT FOR THE
NEW DOCK ON THE RIVER RIBBLE.

'Tis five-and twenty years to day,
  Dear wife, since you and I
Began our life as man and wife:
  Dear me, how time does fly.

It only seems like yesterday,
  When we stood side by side,
In that old church one bright May morn,
  And you became my bride.

We started life in hope and love,
  And all seemed fair and bright ;
But many are the visions that
  Have faded from our sight.

We've had our ups and downs, dear wife,
  And many a trouble sore ;
But when we come to reckon up,
  The blessings have been more.

For when we lost our little Sue,
  Our hearts were sorely grieved ;
But then, she was not all we had,
  We were not quite bereaved.

We've had good health and been content,
  With what of worldly store,
Hath been allotted as our part,
  And never craved for more.

The five-and-twenty years have changed
  Your graceful girlish form,
To one of comely matronhood,—
  To me an added charm.

Our sons and daughters try to cheer,
  And bless our home, dear wife ;
As down the hill from year to year,
  We journey on through life.

We've done our best to train them up
  In wisdom's pleasant way ;
And we are told in after-life,
  Their footsteps will not stray.

Some of them are to manhood grown,
  And left the parent nest ;
Have homes and children of their own,
  With health and comfort blest.

I've asked them all to meet us here
  To celebrate this day ;
And at its close, before we part,
  We'll join in praise, and pray—

That God will bless our goings out,
  And all our comings in ;
That all our words, and deeds, and thoughts,
  Be pure and free from sin.

And thank Him for His mercies too,
  Through all these many years ;
We have not found this world to be
  Always a vale of tears.

For when dark clouds of sorrow roll,
   We've never failed to find,
Howe'er stormy they may be,
   With silver each is lined.

The world keeps moving on apace,
   And we move with it too ;
Let us be earnest in the race,
   In all that's good and true.

So shall we then lay down to rest,
   When all life's conflicts cease ;
And firm in faith, and hope, and trust, .
   Depart this life in peace.

MAY.

WARBLE forth your songs of praises,
   Oh ! ye minstrels of the grove ;
Sing your sweetest songs ye birdies,
   Chant aloud your happy love.
Fill the woodlands with your music,
   Till the echoes sweet resound ;
In the mazes, where the daisies,
   And the woodbine blossom round.

Sweet wild roses ope your petals,
   Waft your fragrance on the air ;
May is come, oh ! haste to greet her,
   Weave a garland for her hair.
And the meadows spangled over,
   With their cups of shining gold ;
Where the rover seeks the clover,
   To draw honey from each fold.

Little lambs with snow-white fleeces,
　In the pastures sport and play ;
With the lowing cattle revelling
　In the sweetness of the May.
And the cuckoo in the distance,
　Oft repeats his mellow lay ;
And rejoices, with the voices,
　Warbling all the livelong day.

And ye crystal brooks and rivers,
　Ye, too, join the choral song ;
Bring your brightest sweetest waters
　To refresh the merry throng.
Gaily dance along your pathway,
　Singing sweetly as ye go,
O'er the shining pebbles rippling,
　Ever onward bright ye flow.

Forest trees all don your garments
　Of the brightest richest green ;
Let your whisperings be the sweetest,
　When you greet your bonny queen.
Rustle in the bright sun glances,
　Quiver o'er the verdant earth ;
Bluebells springing, and their ringing
　Mingles with the joyous mirth.

Glorious Maytime ! merry Maytime !
　Glad we greet thy coming here ;
Brightest, sweetest, merriest Maytime,
　Gladdest month of all the year.
Hedges white with summer snowwreaths,
　Wild birds warbling all the day ;
Flowers springing, dewdrops clinging,
　Welcome sweet and merry May.

A BRIDE STOOD AT THE ALTAR.

A Temperance Poem, published in "The Temperance Mirror," 1884.

A BRIDE stood at the altar, dressed in gleaming silk and lace,
With looks of love and happiness beaming upon her face ;
The bridegroom was beside her in all his manly pride,
Vowing to love and cherish, and forsake all else beside.
 I saw her at the altar, orange blossoms on her brow,
 She looked so fair and winsome : I think I see her now.

Surrounded by six bridesmaids, arrayed in spotless white,
As the vicar read the service : most impressive was the sight ;
The organ strains were swelling in hymns of prayer and praise,
Bright sunbeams on them falling, foretold them happy days.
 I saw her in her beauty, a gay and happy bride,
 With nothing left to wish for in all the world beside.

He took her to a stately home, a lady rich and grand,
Kind wishes poured upon them from friends on every hand ;
No cloud to mar their happiness, or dim their sunny sky :
We little know the hour when deep sorrow draweth nigh.
 I saw her newly wedded, but I never saw her more,
 With the look of perfect happiness, that sunny morn she wore.

A year has passed, and once again I saw that fair young bride.
Arrayed in costly robes and gems, her husband at her side ;
Amidst a ballroom's giddy throng, of which they formed a part,
She looked up in his sparkling eyes, and gave a sudden start.
 I saw her in her costly robes, but would not see her more,
 With the look of hopeless sadness her beauteous face then wore.

His handsome face was hot and flushed, unmeaning was his smile,
As he staggered with unsteady gait, holding her hand the while ;
The harmonious strains of music fell upon unheeding ears,

For he was steeped in drunkenness, and she was drowned in tears,
  I saw him in his weakness, but I would not see him more,
  For my bosom filled with sadness, for the wife whose heart was
    sore.

When next again I saw that pair, 'twas in a maniac's cell,
Beside the inmate stood a form I knew so passing well ;
Her head was bowed, her form was bent, in misery and woe,
Oh ! who would think the demon drink, could change God's creatures
  so.
  I saw them in their misery, but I never saw them more,
  When next we met, no gems had she, and a widow's weeds she
    wore.

REFLECTIONS ON A VISIT TO ST. JOHN'S COLLEGE, GRIMSARGH, Near PRESTON.

A RIGHT happy party we entered the chase
With joy in each heart, and a smile on each face ;
As we drove through the beautiful country lanes :
We forgot for a time all trouble and pains.

We were bound for St. John's, to witness the sports ;
There were handicap races, and games of all sorts ;
And when the band played its inspiriting strains,
We enjoyed the rich treat in those lovely domains.

Warm was our welcome, as we entered the hall,
From the hostess and host, and young students all,
As they ushered us in at the portal so wide,—
In their beautiful home they felt a great pride.

When in the oak chamber we sat down to rest,—
Unique in its beauty by all there confess't,—
We thought noble knights might have dwelt in those halls,
And there held their banquets, receptions, and balls.

We thought of great heroes, so loyal and grand,
Who, for sheltering their king had to forfeit their land ;
In those chambers and grounds a monarch might hide,
And from his enemies securely abide.

We thought of the squires and dames of lang-syne,
Who sat in those chambers, and quaffed off their wine ;
Of weary ones, tired of the world's care and strife,
Who there sought and found peace, all the rest of their life.

We thought of the revels, the dance, and the jest,
When old Father Christmas made welcome each guest ;
When the walls were bedecked with holly and yew,
And from the hall roof hung the mistletoe bough.

When the gay rooms echoed with music and mirth,
And the wassail went round, as bright glowed the hearth,
When the yule log was burned, as it reared in the grate,
With the song and the dance, each heart was elate.

Now all is changed, a spirit reigns there,
Whose presence is seen and felt everywhere ;
Earnestly sowing his seed in the field,
That in God's good time a rich harvest will yield.

We entered the church with its gables so quaint,
Adorned with bright angels and glorified saint ;
Our hearts were all stirred with celestial fire,
As the beautiful anthems were sung by the choir.

The Pastor exhorted the youths in his care,
Of snares and temptations to always beware ;
And never to cause their dear parents a tear,
But always to act as if they were near.

He begged of them all to remember their prayers,
Morning and evening in all their affairs ;
To seek their Creator now in their youth,
And never depart from honour and truth.

As homeward we sped, the theme of each guest,
Was not of the hospitable welcome repast ;
But of that beautiful, bright college home,
Its fame is renouned wherever we roam.

The garden so lovely with rich fruit and flowers,
Called back our minds to Eden's fair bowers ;
And the sweet little brooklet that runs in the dell,
Completes the fair scene with its musical swell.

The thrush's sweet song is heard all around,
From out the woodlands we heard it resound ;
And in the garden among the green bowers,
Melodious and sweet they sing at all hours.

The birds of rich plumage, that roost in the trees,
Remind us af tropical lands o'er the seas ;
And the miniature waterfall toils night and day,
To keep pure the bath, where the youths swim and play.

In luxuriant beauty tall ferns abound,
Where sits the old mandarin* gazing around ;
Not a sound to be heard but the bird and the bee,
And the brook as it sings on its way to the sea.

May the lessons there taught, take root in each heart,
That when from that home they are called to depart ;
They will keep in the path of honour and truth,
As a debt to be paid to the guide of their youth.

*A marble figure.

LAMENT OF THE COUNTESS OF LEICESTER IN CUMNOR CASTLE.

SUGGESTED BY THE SAD MEANING OF THE WORDS, "ALONE! GONE, AND NEVER MORE."

A LADY sat in her chamber,
  So beautiful, noble, and grand,
Lovely and fair were her features.
  And like a white lily her hand ;
Her long thick tresses were braided :
  And like a bright coronet of gold,
Round her small shapely head were twisted
  In many a wondrous fold.

Her form was both tall and stately,
  Her every movement was grace ;
But there was a yearning sadness
  In her fair and beautiful face.
A yearning for something wanting,
  In her large lustrous eyes there beamed,
As she sat in her shining garments
  Like a fair bright vision she seemed.

Unperceived I entered her chamber,
  And gazed on her beauty spellbound,
I saw that her lips were moving,
  And there issued a sweet low sound.
For her words I eagerly listened,
  Wondering what her sorrow could be,
So beautiful rich and noble,
  Yet pining in sad misery.

Her low silvery tones came stealing,
  And fell on my listening ear ;
A world of pathos was in them,
  But they sounded distinct and clear.

They came with such deep sad meauing,
　I remembered them every word :
And this was the cause of sorrow
　From the lady I overheard :

" Oh, what to me is the splendour
　Of all that surrounds me here,
Without a friend to console me,
　Or chase the unbidden tear ?
Is it for this I have bartered
　The love of my father and home,
To pine here in this old castle,
　So weary, sad, and alone ?

Alone ! what a desolate feeling
　That word to my heart now conveys !
Alone ! I knew not its meaning
　In the byegone once happy days,
When we roamed o'er the hills and meadows
　Free as the birds in the air,
And gathered the sweet wild flowers
　That grew round us everywhere.

How dearly I prized the wild roses,
　Because they were plucked by him,
But the thorns now pierce my bosom
　Till my eyes with tears become dim :
These walls to me are a dungeon,
　These jewels are fetters that gall,
And these pearls in my hair are a mockery :
　I'm weary and tired of them all.

To be deck'd out in these baubles,
　With no one to see what I wear ;
I was happier far with my father,
　When I wore a rosebud in my hair.

But I still love him so dearly,
   He is all in the world to me :
I could live in his presence only,
   Alas ! nevermore, can it be.
Gone ! from my life is the sunshine,
   Gone ! is the trust of my youth :
And with them my peace for ever,
   Alone, will my heart be till death."

A MERRY HEART.

A MERRY heart, a merry heart, it shines upon the face,
And insures you a welcome at every time and place :
Like the bright and glowing sunshine, it cheers all around,
And dispenses joy and gladness wherever it is found.

A merry heart is better than gold or precious stones,
Its possessor may be happier than they who sit on thrones;
And with good health united, need envy no man's lot,
Tho' their home may be a palace, and he only has a cot

Cultivate a merry heart, you'll always have a feast,
Rich as any alderman, or shaven monk or priest :
For he who owns a merry heart is richer than a king,
And none can ever rob him of that good and precious thing.

A merry heart with beauty your countenance will grace.
And inspire you with courage to run life's up-hill race :
It will cheer you on the journey, and make you many friends,
For on a light and cheerful heart, our happiness depends.

And a merry heart will give you, more length of days you'll find,
For nothing is so healthful as a cheerful happy mind ;
Its the best of all companions, wherever you may be,
Dull care and melancholy from its presence quickly flee.

SPRING.

Hail ! all hail to beautiful spring,
O'er the hills she comes like a fairy thing ;
Rays of bright sunshine gleam in her hair,
She flits about, so lovely and fair.
And with magic touch awakes from sleep,
The flowers and buds that so slily peep,
From the beds where they have rested long,
Waiting the call of her gladsome song.
They feel the warmth of her sunny beam,
And come forth as from a pleasant dream ;
She lets loose the frost-bound streams that pour,
Refreshing and sweet, through the earth once more.
The lark feels her touch, and with dewy wing
Soars to the clouds singing praise to spring ;
The merry thrush, in the forest dell,
Greets the sweet mate that he loves so well.
The swallows come from their haunts afar,
Led by an unseen guiding star,
To their home beneath the old barn eaves,
Quite safe and secure from boyish thieves.
Oh, lovely spring, so welcome to all,
The flowers unfold at the warmth of thy call ;
The primrose springs in the forest glade,
And blue-bells wave in the silent shade.
The cuckoo's call o'er the fields resound,
All linger to hear the welcome sound ;
And the soft sweet zephyrs gently play,
Around each fluted unfolding spray :
And woo them forth to dance in the rays
Of genial spring, and bright summer days ;
Oh, fair bright spring, how we love thy birth,
Thou comest each year, to make glad the earth.

THE HOLLY.

Oh, the holly ; oh, the holly, how its scarlet berries gleam,
From amid the clustering branches of brightest, richest green ;
Bedeck'd with crystal snow-wreaths, white as foam upon the sea,
Oh, the bright and shining holly, and its berries red for me.

Not a flower in our gardens, or meadows now appear,
To grace the festive season that comes but once a year ;
But the bright and shining holly, with its berries scarlet red,
Old Father Christmas twines, in a garland round his head.

In every hall and castle are the holly branches hung,
When the brimming cup goes round, and the jovial song is sung ;
When the Christmas log is burning upon the glowing hearth,
The holly branch and mistletoe, increase the festive mirth.

The ivy leaves are beautiful, but serve us to remind,
That it revels amid ruin, and is with it oft entwined ;
But the bright and shining holly in meadow land or bower,
Displays its glowing beauty most in the stern winter hour.

The fir tree and the cyprus, and yew tree, too, are fine,
To decorate our parterres, not in our homes to shine ;
They bear no fruit or flowers, and are gloomy, dark, and sad ;
But the bright and shining holly makes our hearts and spirits glad.

Then let us pledge the holly with its berries scarlet red,
Gleaming in rich beauty when the yule log light is shed ;
And the hearts that gather round it, right merry may they be.
When joining in the dance and song, of Christmas revelry.

WINTER.

OLD winter has come, we hear once again
His voice in the wind as it sweeps o'er the plain ;
The aged and poor at his coming despair,
For scant is their clothing and hard is their fare.
But he brings his good gifts to scatter around,
Gladness and mirth in his presence abound :
Music and singing,—joyously ringing,
In castle and cottage is heard to resound

He flings o'er the earth his white mantle of snow,
To nourish the seed which the husbandmen sow ;
He brings his great storm-winds the pestilence to chase,--
To the aged and poor he may wear a stern face.
But he opens the hearts of the rich in the land,
To give of their stores with a bounteous hand ;
Turning their sadness to smiles of gladness,
Uniting earth's children in charity's bond.

What pleasure so great as to ride in a sledge,
When the white snow is drifted high as the hedge ;
The bell's merry tinkle on the clear frosty air,
Enliven the spirits and drive away care.
The beautiful snow like the foam of the sea,
Happy children snowballing we everywhere see ;
As balls they're throwing, their laughters echoing,—
Joyous and gladsome o'er the snow covered lea.

No longer we hear the sweet song of the thrush,
To his mate as she sits on her nest in the bush ;
Nor the lark's song of praise as he soars up on high,
Till he seems like a speck in the blue arching sky.

But more dear than the thrush, or the lark's warbling trill,
Is the little redbreast on the snow covered sill ;
His song is so cheering, we love his appearing,
Other birds are all silent, but he sings on still.

Winter is welcome to youth most of all,
For then is the time for party and ball ;
At no other season do they ever find,
So much recreation that pleases their mind.
Young men and maidens their way they all wend,
With skates on their arms to the lake or the pond ;
So happy and merry, cheeks bright as a cherry,
They glide round the pond a gay lighthearted band.

Then welcome old winter again to our shores,
When rain falls in torrents, and wind loudly roars ;
We'll heap on more wood to keep out the chill,
And read, work, or play, with hearty good will.
Gay garlands we'll weave to twine round his face,
Sadness and gloom from our hearths we will chase ;
Our hearts lightly bounding, and dear friends surrounding,
Old winter is welcome our circle to grace.

TO THE DAISY.

PRETTY flower with golden eye,
Looking upward to the sky,
Heedless of the storms that fly
      Across thy path.

Fields are spangled thickly o'er
With thy tiny modest flower,
E're the sun hath gained the power
      To give thee warmth.

But still thy petals doth expand,
Like stars of hope o'er all the land,
To tell us spring is near at hand
   To clothe the bowers.

Primroses soon will peep from out
Their verdant bed and look about ;
And seeing thee will have no doubt
   'Tis time to rise.

The merry thrush in song so sweet
Will hasten soon his mate to greet :
And to his side with wing so fleet,
   She'll quickly fly.

And skylark soon with dewy breast,
Among thy buds will build her nest ;
And lapwing with his sable vest,
   Will hover near.

The dewdrops nestle on thy lips,
And in the sun their rosy tips
Sparkle like precious amythists,
   Or other gems.

For thee the children leave their games,
And ramble in the fields and lanes,—
To seek thy blooms for daisy chains,
   With keen delight.

And when the summer warmth is past,
Thou brav'st the winter's chilling blast,
Which o'er thy head sweeps fierce and fast,
   With courage still.

RESIGNATION.

"THESE ARE THEY WHICH CAME OUT OF GREAT TRIBULATION."

Cease, my spirit, cease repining,
    Why cast down with bitter woe ;
'Tis the crucible refining,
    To come forth with brighter glow.
Afflictions are but for a moment
    Sent by a kind Father's hand ;
We must pass through tribulation ,
    Ere we join the glorious band.

Trust in the eternal promise —
    He hath said : I will not leave
Those who call on me in trouble ;
    Courage, then, why dost thou grieve.
When all earthly friends deceive thee
    Be not weary or cast down ;
Take thy cross without repining,
    If thou would'st attain the crown.

And for ever serve and worship
    In His temple day and night,
With the shining ones around Him,
 *   In bright robes of spotless white.
Never hungering, never thirsting,
    Never burden'd with great heat :
Singing holy songs of Zion,
    Round the heavenly mercy seat.

THE SONG OF THE WEAVER.

WITH the lark in the early morning, I rise, and away, away,—
Not where the wild flowers are blooming, but where the woof and
   shuttle play ;
They flit to and fro so gaily, and their music is sweet to me,
Far sweeter than songs of the wild birds, or hum of the roving bee.

CHORUS :

Oh ! the merry shuttles click-clacking, is music so sweet to me,
That neither the bee nor the song-birds, can vie with its
   melody.

The woof and the shuttle are toiling, for me all the livelong day,
As I watch the threads they are weaving, I sing—for my heart is
   gay ;
The flowers that I see fashioning, with the the shuttle and loom I
   tend,
Diffuse no fragrant perfume, but flourish for a glorious end.

The flowers in the field will wither, and fade like a morning dream ;
But those that the shuttle weaveth, we can tightly press on the
   beam ;
They clothe the naked and hungry—they feed if they'll toil and
   spin,—
Oh ! the woof and the shuttle right bravely, assist us our bread
   to win.

The woof and shuttle are humble, but a power in Briton's fair Isle,
Silence their merry click-clacking, and millions would cease to
   smile.
Then hurrah for the woof and shuttle, tho' humble be their degree,
Britannia can ill spare the measure, of their click-clacking harmony.

A POEM ON TEA.

PUBLISHED IN "MELIA'S MAGAZINE."

WHAT is it I should like to know,
That makes your cheeks so richly glow
Your heart with cheerfulness o'erflow,
          Tea.

What is it makes your eyes so bright,
Your carriage graceful and upright?
Your healthful spirits always light :
          Tea.

What makes you always free from care,
Sunshine surrounds you everywhere,
All say you are divinely fair?
          Tea.

What is it makes your voice so sweet,
To hear you sing is such a treat,
It almost lifts one off their feet?
          Tea.

I once was often very sad,
And in the mornings always bad,
The elixir which makes me now feel glad
          Is tea.

It cheers the heart and soothes the brain,
And makes the old feel young again,
And in their head they feel no pain
          From tea.

No nectar from the fairy bowers,
Or essence sweet from odorous flowers,
Can vie with the reviving powers
          Of tea.

It is so cheap, the cost is small,
And that will please you most of all,
So go at once and make a call.

     For tea.

And if you value length of days,
Would win the world's admiring gaze,
You've only a few pence to raise,

     For tea.

THE DYING CHILD.

Hush, and tread softly, a spirit is passing
 Through the dark vale to the regions of light ;
Where neither sickness nor sorrow can enter,—
 Bright angels are waiting its aerial flight.

Our sweet little blossom unfolding its beauty,
 Disclosed new tints on each opening morn ;
Oh, how we tended our dear little treasure,—
 But ah, the most beauteous rose has a thorn.

Ere it expanded in full glowing beauty,
 We saw it sickening, each day more and more :
Oh, the anguish we felt when told the destroyer,
 Had fastened its fangs, and was eating its core.

But amidst others resplendent in beauty,
 Our sweet little blossom will bloom now for aye ;
It is not lost, but only transplanted,
 To bloom where no blight can harm or destroy.

MEMORIES OF HOME.

I LIVE in the midst of a city,
    Among all its turmoil and din ;
Among all its joys and sorrows,—
    Its pleasures, temptations, and sin.
But often my thoughts back are flying
    To the home of my youthful days ;
The old farm house in the meadows,
    And its inmates' primitive ways.

I see now its old-fashioned gables,
    And ivy-clad quaint rustic porch ;
Roses adorning the casements,
    Near which grows a tall silver birch.
By the gate a laburnum is waving
    Its bright drooping tassels of gold ;
And Gyp, the petted gray pony,
    Stands by the barn door in the fold.

In fancy I hear the kine lowing ;
    The lambs' plaintive bleat on the moor ;
See the tortoise-shell cat in the window,
    And the house-dog sat at the door.
In the garden wallflowers are growing,
    And hollyhocks stately and tall ;
And sweetbriar hedges are throwing
    Their odorous perfume o'er all.

But dearest of all the home pictures
    Is one with a kind earnest face,—
Imparting words of instruction,
    To prepare me for life's hard race.

And when my heart feels sad and lonely,
  I think of that dearly loved home,
As I toil in the din of the city,
  Or sit in my chamber, alone.

Thinking of heather clad mountains,
  Flow'ry meadows and babbling streams ;
The songs of birds in the dingles,
  Which I now hear only in dreams.
Dreams of the past now engraven,
  On memory while life shall last ;
A memory to bless and cheer me,
  Is thoughts of my life in the past.

LIVE IN LOVE.

Live in love ; tis beautiful to see
A home where all is peace and harmony :
Where angry passions never mar their joy,
But peace and love their hearts and tongues employ

Live in love ; and let no unkind word
Proceeding from your lips be ever heard ;
Kind words like genial showers, often fall
With soothing influence on the minds of all.

Live in love ; let all your actions be
Open as day, clothed in humility ;
And like the violet in its humble bed,
Fragrance around your presence will be shed

OLD MEMORIES.

I REMEMBER, I remember, when a happy child I played,
And roamed with Dash and Willie in the meadow and the glade !
Wild and free and happy as the birds upon the bough,—
The memory of those hours are a blessing to me now.

My pinafore oft draggled with playing in the brook,
And when of that we tired, we sat in some shady nook ;
O joyous was my childhood, as I roamed across the lea,
And lived in the old homestead, with my father, Farmer Lee.

We gathered sweet wild flowers in fields and shady lanes,
Chased the bees and butterflies, and wove bright daisy chains :
The memory of those hours of my being form a part,—
For they are now engraven in gold letters on my heart.

And how well I remember when my childhood had passed by,
We still loved our favourite rambles, Willie, Dash, and I ;
Willie brought me oft a flower, which I nursed with loving care,
And sometimes a pretty ribband, which he tied around my hair.

We always went on Sunday to the little village church,
And at the close of service, Willie lingered in the porch ;
He came with hand outstretched and such a happy smile,
To escort me o'er the meadows, and converse a little while.

He brought me now a book where he used to bring a toy,
And I think somehow or other it gave me greater joy ;
Always when I heard his footsteps it made my heart so glad.—
I knew he came to see me : that blithe and bonny lad.

I felt my eyes grow brighter, and my cheeks a rosy red,
As I listened with sweet pleasure to every word he said ;
But a day came when we parted, he left his native land,
And before we separated I promised him my hand.

Oh, how I watched the vessel, as she rode across the foam,
Taking all the sunshine from my heart and from my home ;
The days were long and lonely, but I tried to think that soon,
Willie would come back again, and claim me for his own.

But days and weeks passed over, and I got no word from him ;
My spirit lost its lightness, and my cheeks became quite thin ;
Oh, how I hoped and waited, and longed for his return,
Till my heart grew sad and lonely, for no tidings could I learn.

At length I lost my father, and I then went far away,
Unto a distant city, with a relative to stay ;
But tho' in a crowded city I felt so sad and lone,—
And the heart within my bosom, became heavy as a stone.

I am now an aged woman ; alone, with snow-white hair ;
Oh, how I long to visit my childhood's home once more,
Where I spent my happy girlhood, and my father lies at rest,—
Endeared to my memory, by the sweet and happy past.

LINES ADDRESSED TO PENWORTHAM CHURCH.
NEAR PRESTON.

Noble old pile, how oft I stop to gaze
On thy gray walls that echo with glad praise ;
When organ strains and voices sweetly blend.
As rich and poor with lowly reverence bend.
Ages that eminence thou hast proudly graced,
Thy beauty not diminished, or defaced.
O'erlooking vales, where nature richly showered
Her fairest gifts, and now thou art embowered
In shelt'ring trees, that shield thee from the blast
Of winter storms, that beat so loud and fast ;

But thy square tower, with clinging ivy clad,
Peeps through the waving branches, as if glad
To view again the fertile vales below,
Through which the Ribble's streams still gently flow,
Forever meandering onward to the sea,
'Mid verdant slopes o'ertopped with forest tree,
And sylvan dells where wild birds sweetly sing,
Proclaiming the first breathings of the spring,
And summer noonday in the leafy glades :
Their joyous music the soft air pervades.
Thy silvery chimes float o'er the flowing tide,
Resounding through the vale from side to side.
Sometimes we hear their sad and mournful knells.
A tale of woe and grief their pealing tells.
A many changes round thee hath there been
Since first thy walls o'erlooked the charming scene :
When fruitful orchards smiling were displayed
Where now the marsh, a desert waste, is laid,
And cottage homes for thousands have been reared
Within thy range since thou at first appeared.
But north, and south, and west are still the same
As when thou first received thy honoured name ;
When monks and pilgrims trod thy lonely aisles,
Telling their beads, unheeding nature's smiles.

Many who from youth have met and prayed,
In thy lone graveyard now in peace are laid ;
Until they rise at the last trumpet sound,
Their tombs encircle thy gray walls around.
Father and mother, daughter, too, and son.
Are gathered to thy bosom one by one.
The sable rooks a requiem o'er them sing,
Awaking echoes with their caw-cawing :

They make their homes upon the branches high,
Fearless of hurricanes that o'er them fly :
The deep solemnity that round thee reigns
Is suited to their habits and their aims.
A beacon light upon the hill thou art,
Inspiring hope in many a soul-sick heart.
The noble oaks and beeches side by side,
That form thy grand old avenue long and wide,—
A king might covet, for his palace home,—
We seldom see its like where'er we roam.
And in the woodlands sweet wild flowers abound,
Unseen they bloom, in silence so profound ;
Nature's most beauteous charms around thee shine,
The privilege to enjoy them all is mine.

A FLORAL BOUQUET.

You may sing of the roses, and all sorts of posies,
    Of sweet scented violets all sparkling with dew ;
Heartsease and lilies that grow in the valleys,
    Sweet pinks, and carnations, and bells of sky-blue.

Of buttercups and daisies, you're loud in their praises,
    Of daffodils, cowslips, and sweet eglantine ;
But the pale primrose that blooms 'neath the hedgerows,
    To me all the others its blossoms outshine.

In youth and in childhood, I roamed in the wild wood,
    To gather its blooms in the early spring day ;
Fond those recollections, and sweet the reflections,
    Of those scenes of my youth with friends far away.

THE WOOD NYMPH.

I sat on a stile in the meadows one morning,
    Listening to the lark as he sang loud and high ;
When a maiden approached me, looking so charming.
    And said " if you please, will you let me pass by."

Her voice it was sweet, as the summer winds sighing,
    But it made my heart beat, I could hear its pit-pat :
I thought her a nymph, or a fairy, just trying
    Her magical spells upon me as I sat.

I gazed on the vision of beauty in wonder
    If it was mortal, or a spirit of air ;
With an effort I broke the spell I was under,
    And saw it was only a maiden stood there.

Bright as the dew-drops her dark eyes were gleaming,
    And pure as wild roses, the bloom on her cheek ;
Her face was so winsome, with tender smiles beaming,
    That soon I recovered, and ventured to speak.

I said, " fairest maiden, a bride I am seeking,
    I seek one that's loving, kind, tender, and true :
My heart is so wildly with love for you beating,
    It tells me kind fate's sent me hither to you.

You shall dwell in a mansion in London city,
    And ride in a carriage, in costly array."
Her eyes beamed with laughter, she said " What a pity
    My husband can't hear you, he's coming this way."

DAY-BREAK.

WITH gladness we greet thee, goddess of morning,
  Thou comest in glory to light up the earth ;
The twinkling stars to their homes are returning,
  Abash'd at thy glorious splendour and mirth.
The great orb of day ascends o'er the mountains,
  In beautiful raiment of crimson and gold ;
Reflecting his hues on rivers and fountains,
  As onward they glide over meadow and wold.

And at thy coming the mists are all clearing,
  Like a curtain unfolding thy glories to show ;
Filmy-winged insects in myriads appearing,
  Gyrate in the beams of the bright morning's glow.
Sweet feather'd minstrels rejoice at thy coming,
  And haste to salute thee with songs of glad praise ;
Wild bees in delight, round the flowers are humming,
  As they gently unfold in the warmth of thy rays.

The cock's clarion voice is loudly proclaiming,
  He welcomes thy coming, and greets thee with joy ;
And skylark in ecstacy, earth is disdaining,
  And is warbling and winging his way to the sky.
Oe'r the green meadows the milkmaid trips lightly,
  Her feet scarcely brush from the daisies the dew ;
She calls to the kine—her voice sweet and sprightly,—
  With lowing they greet her, and follow her too.

The cuckoo's soft notes resound o'er the meadows,
  And red clover blossoms diffuse their perfume ;
O'er the narrow green lanes, where the flickering shadows,
  Wave o'er the sweet hawthorn, and eglantine's bloom.

Goddess of morning, all greet thee with gladness,
   We rejoice in thy beauty, thy brightness and mirth ;
When thou returnest, all silence and sadness,
   Is banished in the joy of the new morning's birth.

LOVE'S INFLUENCE.

Oh love, sweetest love, how shall I woo thee,
   Come to my bosom and rest there for aye ;
Sweet is thy presence, let me enfold thee,
   To my lone heart, there forever to lie.
Come love, sweet love, oh come let me woo thee,
   To my lone heart, to rest there for aye.

Thine is the charm to chase away sadness,
   Thine is the balm for the heart's bitter woe ;
Thine is the power to impart joy and gladness,
   Greater than riches or titles bestow.
Come love, sweet love, oh come let me woo thee,
   To my lone heart, to rest there for aye.

Without thee a palace were gloomy and cheerless,
   A cottage is heaven if blest with thy smiles ;
Patient, enduring, gentle yet fearless,
   A safeguard thou art, from temptations' wiles.
Come love, sweet love, oh come let me woo thee,
   To my lone heart, there forever to lie.

I'LL THINK OF THEE.

When the early morning sunbeams
　Rise to gladden all the earth,
Gilding mountain, hill, and valley,—
　Filling all with joy and mirth ;
When the skylark soaring upward,
　Sings his morning song of praise ;
And the linnet, thrush, and blackbird
　Warble forth their happy lays :
　　　　　　　　I'll think of thee.

When the noontide is advancing,
　And I seek the leafy bowers ;
Nature's sounds my soul entrancing,
　As I sit among the flowers.
When wild bees are gathering honey
　From the rose and lily's cup ;
And the lowing herds of cattle
　From the running waters sip :
　　　　　　　　I'll think of thee.

When the day is fast declining,
　And all nature seeks repose ;
When the clear pale moon is shining,
　And with soft refulgence glows ;
When the nightingale is singing
　On the greenwood's forest tree ;
And the evening breeze is bringing
　Mingled sounds of melody :
　　　　　　　　I'll think of thee.

In the deep and silent watches
  Of the solemn midnight hour,
When all's locked in deepest slumber,
  Guarded by Almighty power.
In my dreams I'm ever with thee,
  Hand in hand, and heart to heart ;
Then I feel thy presence near me,
  And I dread that we should part :
              In dreams of thee.

THE PATRIOT'S FAREWELL TO ERIN.

Erin, dear Erin, must I leave thee for ever,
  Beautiful Erin, sweet land of my birth :
Nevermore wander o'er thy blue mountains,
  Or gaze with delight on thy emerald earth ?

No more shall I hear the sweet harp of my country,
  No more its loved notes my spirit beguile ;
But in my heart its sweet tones will linger,
  When far, far away, from Erin's green isle.

Farewell to the little white cot in the valley,
  Its quaint porch and lattice, with roses entwined ;
Endeared by a thousand fond recollections,
  Is that loved spot I am leaving behind.

But tho' I must leave you, sweet home and dear Erin,
  Enshrined in my heart for ever you'll be :
And in my wanderings, my greatest endeavour
  Will be to gain freedom, dear Erin for thee.

IN MEMORIAM.

TO THE LATE P.M. 314: LATE P P.G., S. OF W.; P.G.S.W,

AND is he gone? he, whom we have seen so lately
In manhood's prime : his form so tall and stately,
With genial smile, so cheerful and refined,
Welcomed by all, his great and lofty mind
With endless fund of wit and wisdom stored ;
Envied by some, by all who knew him best, adored.
Proud of his race, and of his high estate,—
Deceit and wrong incurred his deepest hate.
A mind attuned to sweet harmonious sounds :
His love for music scarcely knew its bounds.
On youthful sports he looked with boyish glee :
His soul was filled with heaven-born charity.
Deserving cases ne'er appealed in vain ;
But woe to him who would by fraud obtain.
The withering glance that shot from eye and brow,
Gave warning he had read the knave right through.
He journey'd far to forward the great cause*,
That soothes the widows' and the orphans' woes.
Though oft in need of rest for mind and limb,
Till duty done, there was no rest for him.
He went his way : not looking right nor left,
Till like a tree with scathing lightning cleft.
But now he rests without a care or pain :
His loss to us, may be his greatest gain ;
He rests in peace until the judgment day.—
May we then see him clothed in bright array :
Not earthly jewels,† but a glorious crown,
Though without warning he was smitten down :
To realms of bliss triumphant may he rise
His wondering spirit fill d with glad surprise.

          * Freemasoury.   † Masonic.

THE WITHERED ROSE-BUD.

I FOUND a withered rose-bud among my treasures rare,
That rose-bud I once cherished with tender loving care;
'Twas given as a token of constancy and trust,
I felt no thorn upon it when I wore it in my breast.

I placed it in my chamber, and watched it with great pride,
Unfold its beauteous blossoms e'er it withered, drooped, and died;
I thought its glowing brightness an emblem of my life,
When he who was the giver, came to claim me as his wife.

But as its beauty withered, the thorns then came in view,
And I knew he who gave it, had proved to me untrue:
Both sharp they were and bitter, they pierced my very heart,—
But another sweet fresh rosebud, soon healed the painful smart.

INCONSTANCY.

I'VE been thinking, darling Johnnie,
　　When you first made love to me,
Of the glances that you gave me
　　From the corner of your e'e;
How they set my heart a'beating,
　　I am sure you never knew;
If you had you surely would
　　Have been more kind and true.

And how you used to linger,
　　By the side of that old stile,
When I left you to go home,
　　Tho' you had to walk a mile.

I thought you loved me dearly,
  And I was so happy then ;
But I since have found it out
  You are like all other men.

And they are like the butterflies,
  That rove from flower to flower ;
Sipping all the sweetness
  In the bright and sunny hour.
But when tempests gather,
  They are never to be seen ;
Tho' the flower hath the beauty
  And the graces of a queen.

THE SAILOR'S RETURN.

OVER the ocean my Jammie's been roaming,
  A blithe sailor laddie is he ;
His heart is so light, and smile is so winning,
  And black as the sloe is his e'e.
How sad was the day when from me he parted :
  I strove hard my feelings to hide ;
And tried to look gay, when he went away,
  Until the ship's anchor was weigh'd.

Then fast down my cheeks the tears began streaming,
  As the ship rode out of the bay ;
I felt in my heart as if I was dreaming,
  And turned with a sad heart away.
But now he's returning, and happy we'll be,
  My glad heart is singing with joy ;
And gay as the thrush, that sings in the bush,
  I'll welcome my blithe sailor boy.

MY SOLDIER BOY.

PUBLISHED IN THE "FAMILY HERALD."

My heart's more light and gladsome,
　　Than its been for many a day ;
I ll don my gown of sarcenet,
　　Deck my hair with ribbons gay.
The cruel wars are over,
　　I'll dance and sing for joy ;
For Johnnie's coming home again,
　　My brave bright soldier boy.

My Johnnie's tall and handsome,
　　So loving, kind, and true :
The sunshine all departed
　　From my life, when first I knew
He wished to be a soldier,
　　And cross the deep wide sea.
But now the wars are over,
　　He's coming home to me.

My many prayers are answered,
　　My Johnnie's spared to me :
Amid the din of battle,
　　And the shouts of victory.
One heard my supplication :
　　Turned my mourning into joy,
By sending back my darling,
　　My noble soldier boy.

THE CLOUD WITH THE SILVER LINING.

Come, dry up your tears, my darling,
　Don't grieve for my going away :
I'll soon return to you, darling,
　And be happy as thrushes in May.
Leave off those tears and repinings,
　And strive to be cheerful in mind :
For every dark cloud of sorrow,
　With a streak of bright silver is lined.

Keep up your courage, my darling,
　Put all sad forebodings away :
After night joy comes in the morning,
　And turns out a sunshiny day.
Remember past blessings, my darling,
　For we've always been able to find,
That every dark storm-cloud of sorrow
　With a streak of bright silver is lined.

Now I must leave you, my darling,
　I shall soon be across the wide sea :
But my heart will ever be yearning,
　To come back, my darling, to thee.
Now kiss me good-bye and be happy,
　And always keep this in your mind :
That every dark storm-cloud of sorrow,
　With a streak of bright silver is lined.

LILY.

On ! there is pretty Lily,
I'll go to her willy-nilly,
In the garden where she's singing,
And like silver bells when ringing,
        Is her voice so sweet.

CHORUS—

Oh ! isn't it very funny, like a bee when gathering honey,
She does not care for money, she's so very sweet on me.

Her namesake is not fairer,
No rose is any rarer ;
Than her cheek so rich and blooming,
In the garden where she's roaming,
        With her step so light.

Her eyes like stars are shining,
Her golden curls she's twining,
Round and round her pretty fingers,
As she looks around and lingers,
        She's thinking of me.

I will no longer tarry,
But ask her if she'll marry ;
I've a little home so charming,
I'll propose to her this morning,
        To share it with me.

MAY-DAY.

WELCOME May-day ! with its brightness,
Filling all with joy and lightness ;
With the odorous scents of flowers, and the song of happy birds.
Oh ! how every heart rejoices,
When the music of their voices,
Resound from dell and dingle, or when soaring to the clouds.

Glorious May-day ! with what pleasure,
We now wander at our leisure,
When the hedges with blossoms of the fragrant May are crowned ;
And the honeysuckle twining,
Their rich scents the bees divining,
Gaily flit from flower to flower, humming, roving, all around.

Merry May-day ! sunbeams glancing,
On the youths and maidens dancing,
Round the May-pole, at the crowning of their chosen village
queen ;
And the joyous bells are ringing,
Sweetest melody are flinging,
At the revels of the May-day, when dancing on the green.

Happy May-day ! when beholding
Each new beauteous flower unfolding,
In the verdant meadows greening, with the daisies spangled o'er ;
And the drowsy cattle lowing
By the crystal streamlets flowing,
Where the stately velvet rushes wave upon its marshy shore.

BASHFUL NORA.

Come, Nora, me darlin', don't look so shy,
I see by the glance ove yer purty black eye,
Ye mane to say no, and be tazing again,
But I think I'll go back to Biddy M'Shane.

I must have a wife to look afther the pigs,
And the cocks and hins while the pratie's I digs ;
Now, Biddy at once would be glad to say yes,
And I'd not need to ask her to give me a kiss.

And Biddy ye know is a foin hansom girl,
Wid swate rosy cheeks set my heart in a whirl ;
What, Nora Mavourneen, a tear in yer eye,
I was only in fun, yer love, darlint, to thry.

The pigs, the dear critters, would all be so glad,
Wid you for their misthress, the hins too, bedad ;
So come wid me dar.int, away to the priest,
And Biddy M'Shane shall dance at the feast.

A SUMMER EVENING.

You ask if I remember, the time when first we met,
    One lovely summer evening, just when the sun had set ;
In sad reverie I walked alone, when like a vision bright,
    You came upon my musings and filled my soul with light.

You ask if I remember,—as if I could forget
    That long past summer evening, when you and I first met ;
'Twas the dawning of the morning, of a long bright summer day,
    And a glorious evening sunset now beams upon our way.

THE FADED LILY.

It was only a faded lily,
   That I found in the leaves of a book ;
But oh, what feelings came o'er me
   As I took one long lingering look.

Such a rush of fond and sweet memories,
   Came over my lone heart once more :
As I gazed on the faded lily
   In my bosom I once had wore.

I was his promised bride when we parted,
   And wore the sweet flower he had given :
But the grass is now waving o'er him,
   And his gentle spirit in heaven.

CRADLE SONG.

Sleep thee, my darling one, sink thee to rest,
Safe from all harm in thy warm cosy nest ;
Over thy slumbers a watch I will keep,
Singing a lullaby, sleep, darling, sleep.

Sunbeams are sinking away in the west,
And the sweet birdies have all gone to rest ;
The flowers have supped of the dewdrops so bright,
Closed up their petals, and bid all good-night.

Bright stars are peeping out from the skies
To tell us 'tis time to close baby-eyes,
So sleep thee, my darling, sleep thee, my own,
Dreaming of angels till morning shall dawn.

POLLY WATKINS.

I MET her in the meadows and in the village street
Like a ray of sunshine was her glance so bright and sweet ;
Cheeks tinted like the roses, eyes like the summer sky,
For pretty Polly Watkins I oft'n heave a sigh.

CHORUS.

Oh, pretty Polly Watkins, I love her as my life,
But never yet dare ask her if she will be my wife.

I've had my eye on Polly since I met her one fine morn,
When walking in the meadows and feeling quite forlorn ;
She appeared like a vision, and cupid shot his dart,
And since that day has rankled the wound within my heart.

For Polly she is cruel, she bestows her smiles on all,
And one day I saw her talking to a soldier smart and tall ;
Her face suffused with blushes, a bright and rosy red,
I since have felt so wretched, I'd better far be dead.

AILEEN.

AWAKE from thy slumber, come Aileen, awaken,
   The sun o'er the mountains is rising in view ;
A chorus of music the song birds are making,
   And all the sweet flowers are sparkling with dew.

Come haste thee, my darling, thou need'st no adorning,
   Come grace with thy beauty this fair morning scene ;
I long for thy presence, I must be returning,
   So pray thee come quickly, my darling Aileen.

Oh ! why dost thou linger when time's fleeting moments,
    Are passing so fleetly, and I must away ;
Thy presence will chase away all doubting torments,
    As the sun the gray mists at the dawning of day.

I must soon leave thee, but time cannot sever,
    The bonds that unite us, tho' seas roll between :
They are stronger than death, and the ocean will never,
    Quench the love that I bear thee, my darling Aileen.

THE SQUIRE AND THE MAID.

As a brisk young squire was riding to London one fine day,
He saw a pretty young maiden resting beside the way ;
She said, kind sir, will you tell me the way to London town ?
I'm footsore, tired, and weary, but I've heard of its great renown.
I'm going to seek my fortune, I hav'nt a shilling to spend,
And in all the wide world over, not one I can call my friend.

Her eyes were blue as summer skies, and cheeks just like the rose,
Grace in her every movement, tho' poor and shabby her clothes ;
I'll take you there, my dear, he said, if you will come with me,
You shall have gems and silken gowns, and a great lady be ;
And here's a pound to spend, my dear, when you get to the town—
Oh ! thank you sir, the maid replied ; from her eyes the tears fell
    down.

From his horse the squire alighted, with the maiden to sympathize,
When light as a bird she mounted, and rode off before his eyes ;
She kissed her hand, away she flew, with famed John Gilpin's speed
And the squire was left lamenting, the loss of his high-bred steed.
His saddle bags held his pistols, and pouch well filled with gold—
Away with them rode the maiden, who was so handsome and bold.

A MORNING SERENADE.

Arise, love, and come o'er the mountain with me
And soft tales I'll whisper, my darling, to thee ;
Come o'er the mountain, come o'er the hills,
And wander with me by the sweet purling rills.
Dewdrops are gleaming on flower and tree,
But brighter thy eyes will shine, darling, to me,
Come, away love, away, o'er the mountain we'll stray,
Where sweet gentle breezes around us will play.

Come forth from thy chamber ; come, love, let us roam
Where the proud eagles secure make their home,
In the crags of the rocks, o'er the swift rushing streams :
Come, haste thee, my darling, awake from thy dreams.
Sweet is the morning, but sweeter will be
All nature, my darling, when thou art with me ;
Come, away love, away, o'er the mountain we'll stray,
Where sweet gentle breezes around us will play.

MY MARY.

Meet me, my Mary, down the green meadows,
  Where wild roses bloom, and sweet violets spring.
Come in the morning, when dewdrops adorning
  The red clover blossoms, and bees round them sing.

Sweet is the evening, but morning is sweeter,
  When all is waking to gladness and mirth;
Come to me, Mary, oh, haste and come early,
  To see all the brightness and gladness of earth.

When with new beauty flowers are unfolding,
  When with sweet music the wild woodlands ring ;
When nature's voices, in chorus rejoices,
  Our glad hearts, my Mary, too, with them shall sing.

MY NELLY.

OF all the sweet girls in our town
   My Nelly is the sweetest ;
Her eyes are bright, and heart so light
   And footstep is the fleetest.
And Nelly she can play and sing,
   And waltzes so divinely :
I danced with her the other night,
   And she did foot it finely.

But better still, my Nelly has
   A temper of the meekest ;
And she can bake, and she can brew,
   And darn a sock the neatest.
So Nelly is the girl for me,
   If I can only win her;
For every day I then shall be
   Sure of a dainty dinner.

THE FLOWER ON THE WYE.

DOWN the green meadows where cowslips are blowing,
   And golden eyed daisies peep up at the sky :
Where little lambs bleat, and cattle are lowing,
   There stands an old mill on the banks of the Wye.

In that old mill-house a sweet flower is blooming,
   Neither lily nor rose with its beauty can vie ;
I saw her one eve as I walked in the gloaming,
   Near the old mill on the banks of the Wye.

Sweet was her smile as the rosiest May morning,
   Her eyes like the blue of the soft summer sky,
The wild rose's blush her fair cheeks adorning ;
   She has lived in my heart since we met on the Wye.

If I can win this fair lovely blossom,
  So rich in its beauty, to gladden my eye ;
It shall live in my heart, and rest in my bosom :
  Cherished and loved till the day that I die.

THE MILK-MAID.

A MILK-MAID went out from her dairy,
  And tripped on the meadows one morn ;
Her footsteps were light as a fairy,
  And cheeks like the rose on the thorn.
Her face with a sweet smile was lighted,
  As she came to the old rustic stile,
Where vows of true love she had plighted
  To handsome young Charlie O'Lisle.

But Charlie was not there to meet her,
  He'd ne'er been a laggard before :
But always there waiting to greet her,
  And her heart became heavy and sore.
A thrush in the bushes was singing,
  Which greatly increased her dismay ;
She thought that his notes clear and ringing,
  Said, Charlie will not come to-day.

She was turning away, sad and wretched,
  When she heard a quick footstep behind ;
'Twas Charlie, his strong arms outstretched,
  And soon her light form they entwined.
He lovingly chid her for doubting
  (As the thrush kept repeating his lay) ;
Quickly she left off her pouting,
  And the saucy young thrush flew away.

A STORY OF ANTS.

ONCE a famous local preacher
  Of very great renown,
Received a call to preach one day,
  In a far distant town.

He donn'd his best black Sunday coat,
  And hat of softest felt ;
That hat was known by everyone,
  In the place where he dwelt.

He carried nothing but a bag
  To put his sermon in ;
And just a little drop of wine,
  He thought would be no sin.

So off he went quite dignified,
  As parsons ought to be ;
And for the train was just in time,
  And very pleased was he.

Arriving at the junction, he
  Had got an hour to wait,
And that's the reason that I have
  A story to relate.

The junction was a country place,
  Both comfortless and bare ;
He could not find a decent room,
  To sit in anywhere.

The day was beautifully fine,
  He sauntered round about,
To find a quiet resting place,
  Until the time was out.

He saw a verdant meadow near,
    A pathway through it ran ;
And that he thought was just the place,
    His sermon o'er to scan.

So he sat down upon the grass,
    Beneath an old oak tree ;
And soon the hour had passed away,
    And passed right pleasantly.

He saw the train was coming up,
    And hurried to get in ;
He found an empty first, and that
    Was just the thing for him.

So in he got and settled down,—
    He'd drawn the windows up ;
And of his wine quite sparingly,
    He took a little sup

The train began to move, and soon
    The parson he moved too ;
For he could not imagine what
    The dickens was to do.

He looked about upon the seat,
    But could see nothing there ;
Yet such a dreadful tingling
    Was on him everywhere.

He rubb'd, and rubb'd, and rubb'd again,
    But still the smarting grew ;
So he determined he would see
    What with him was to do.

His nether garment he removed,
  And found the bitter cause ;
Upon an ant-hill he had sat :
  They swarmed upon his clothes.

He never was so much perplexed :
  He knew not what to do ;
For fast as he could brush them off,
  The onset they'd renew.

He turned his garment inside out,—
  The dreadful little pests
Were racing up and down, as if
  The fiend had them possessed.

He let the carriage window down,
  With such a savage bang :
He'd quite forgot poor patient Job,
  And all his suffering.

He first look'd this way, then look'd that,—
  Then out he held his pants ;
And how he did anathematise
  Those daring little ants.

He shook, and shook, with all his might,
  As he'd ne'er shook before ;
He little knew when he set out,
  What for him was in store.

For as he drew them in again,
  They slipped from out his hand
And like a bird went fluttering down,
  Alighting on the sand.

In frantic haste he grasp'd the cord,
  To stop the train, — but then
They'd take him for a lunatic,
  And send for policemen.

So he concluded then to wait
  Until the train should stop :
And then upon the platform, he
  From it would quickly drop.

So acting on this wise resolve,
  Until his journey's end,
He sat in silent agony :
  A chaos was his mind.

His journey ended safe at last.
  And quickly out he ran,
Into the waiting room, but not
  The one for gentlemen.

Two maiden ladies in the room
  Sat quite sedate and prim :
But such a scream they both set up.
  When they at first saw him.

The porters, and the master, too,
  All ran to know the cause ;
And then the parson told them all
  The story of his woes.

So they at once supp'ied him with
  Another pair of pants ;
But while he lives he'll ne'er forget
  Those torturing little ants.

BEAUTIFUL RIVER.

BEAUTIFUL river! say where is your home ;
Whence do ye come with your spray and your foam ;
Singing so gaily, sparkling and bright,
Hastening along by day and by night?

Beautiful river! say where do ye go :
What is your purpose and why do ye flow :
Perchance ye may linger sometimes on your way,
But nothing can ever induce you to stay ?

My home was in Eden ; my journey began
When pronounced to be good for the service of man ;
In that beautiful garden I watered the flowers,
When Adam and Eve dwelt in its fair bowers.

I roam over mountains and heather-crowned hills,
Where wild deer come bounding to drink at my rills,
I wind round the plains refreshing and free,
A blessing to all on my way to the sea.

I bound over rocks to the valleys below,
And form a fair scene artists all love to draw ;
Tall ferns and lichens encircle my way,
Drinking beauty and life from my moistening spray.

Through leafy glades where nightingales sing,
And primroses bloom with the first breath of spring ;
Where nature rejoices in jubilant song,
I join the glad chorus when rolling along.

I supply the mill pond so useful and deep,
From whose placid bosom the white lilies peep ;
For the use and the service of all was I given,
Free as the sunlight and pure air of heaven.

TO THE SKYLARK.

SWEET happy songster, soaring on high,
Winging thy way to the beautiful sky ;
What spirit inspires the exquisite lay,
Thou warblest so sweetly all hours of the day?

Is thy home in the corn so happy and bright,
That thou leavest with feelings so full of delight ;
And singest glad praises for joy to thee given,
As nearer and nearer thou soarest to heaven ?

What is the theme of thy glorious lay ?
A fountain of gladness thou pourest all day ;
Many sad hearts are cheer'd by thy strain,
Sing on little bird and cheer them again.

Dull is the earth for a being like thee,
Whose heart is so full of sweet melody ;
Thy mate, from her home, thy voice must admire,
As upward thou springest, higher still higher.

Thou teachest a lesson to man, little bird,
Thou art so grateful for blessings conferr'd ;
Sweet is thy life,—how joyous to see,
Such delight in a thing so tiny as thee.

Sing on, sweet bird ! from the clouds we hear,
Thy song resounding exquisite and clear ;
We think of the angels, thou bright little bird,
And believe their songs, we sometimes have heard.

COME JESSIE.

Come Jessie, come Jessie : oh ! come and away,
Over the meadows where lambs skip and play ;
Where birds sing so gaily in eglantine bowers,
And bees sip the sweets from the dew laden flowers.
Lays soft and sweet as the waters that glide,
I will sing to thee, Jessie : oh ! haste to my side.

The sweet song of the mavis echoes in the glen :
Come Jessie, come Jessie and linger not, when
My bosom is longing to gaze on my queen,
And morning is beaming so bright and serene.
Sunbeams are gleaming o'er earth and o'er sky,
But more bright is the light in thy soft beaming eye.

———————

BERWYN, NORTH WALES.

Lovely Berwyn ! how my heart
Longs for language to impart
To the world thy beauties rare
Which are so surpassing fair.
Glorious mountains towering high,
Reaching almost to the sky ;
Crown'd with purple heather bloom ;
Rich air laden with perfume ;
Golden gorse gleam on the sides,
Where the screaming lapwing hides,
Safely in his mountain home,
Where man's footsteps seldom roam,

On the slopes the feathery pines
Wave their branches near the mines,
That are rich in granite stones,
Where once eagles fixed their thrones,
In the crags above the the vale,
Inaccessible to scale.
On the torrents rushing streams,
Wild and beautiful as dreams ;
Rushing, roaring, night and day,
By their sides the conies play ;
From their bracken hom s they skip,
The tender grass and herbs to nip.
And the shepherd, o'er his sheep,
With his dog a watch doth keep ;
Pipes his reed with sweet content,
Thankful of the blessings sent.
In the vale the dappled herd,
Graze where not a sound is heard ;
But sweet nature's glorious voice,
When the birds and beasts rejoice.
And the rippling murmuring stream,
Famed in song and poet's theme,—
Winding sweetly round the hills.
Ferns and flowers bend o'er its rills,
Mighty oaks o'er-arch its tide ;
And beeches flourish by its side :
Alders bend and willows weep,
O'er its waters clear and deep.
And tall whispering aspens gleam
In the sunlight's glowing beam ;
Flickering rays it brightly throws,
On the streamlet as its flows.
And the church upon its banks,—

Earlier then Llywelyn ranks ;
Centuries its walls have stood,
In that lonely silent wood ;
And the ever flowing Dee,
Adds to its solemnity.
In that church is often heard
Reading from the holy word.
One * whose name both far and wide,
Million hearts revere with pride ;
As they read the pure life o'er,
Of Good Albert, now no more.
Above the church in peace serene,
Stands his home, where late our Queen,
Deign'd to grace that charming vale :
All with pride now tell the tale.

GWENDOLIN, THE MILLER'S DAUGHTER.

By the Dee there lived a miller, and a happy man was he :
Morn, noon, and night, his water-wheel went round so merrily ;
He whistled and he sang all day, and went to bed at night,
In health and sweet contentment, and slept till morning light.

The swish-swash of his water-wheel was music to his ears,
But sweeter still his daughter's voice, a maid of eighteen years ;
Young Gwendolin was fair and bright as any morn in May,
The darling of her father's heart, so happy and so gay.

* Sir Theodore Martin.

She'd lovers plenty, but she turned a deaf ear to them all,
She always was the village belle, at party and at ball ;
She lov'd to climb the mountains, and ramble by the stream,
That of many a song and story has been the pleasant theme.

The speckl'd trout in that fair stream were fam'd for being fine,
And unto anglers it was known, they came in summer time ;
One day a youth of noble mien was sitting by the stream,
And seeing fair Gwendolin, thought her like a poet's dream.

From that time he thought the fishes near the mill were much the
    best,
And daily love for Gwendolin was growing in his breast ;
When he saw her leave the mill, he followed in her wake,
And met her on the mountain, in the meadow, and the brake.

And Gwendolin was so happy as she'd never been before,
Her lover was so handsome, and he told her o'er and o'er
How very much he loved her, quite dearly as his life ;
If she'd consent to marry, she should be his wedded wife.

Her father would not give consent for her to go away,
But the lover he was urgent, said he could no longer stay ;
So he at length consented, the light went from his home,
And somehow, now, the water-wheel had lost its merry tone.

His home was in the city, they lived happy for a while,
But soon she missed the brightness of his gay and pleasant smile ;
And oft till early morning hours, he now would stay away,
She saw that with excitement he was flushed from day to day.

She could not long be ignorant of the sad and bitter cause,
She sometimes remonstrated, and begged of him to pause ;
She thought of her kind father who was now so far away,
And for her husband's weakness, would often kneel and pray.

He lived in the great city, such a gay and restless life,
That Gwendolin often wearied of its hollowness and strife ;
Like a sweet wild flower transplanted in uncongenial soil,
Gwendolin's spirits drooped, but she bore up for a while.

Her husband grew indifferent as he saw her pine and fade,
And left off the attentions he before to her had paid ;
And from indifference soon he grew to words and sometimes blows,
When maddened by excitement that the drunkard only knows.

He drank and gambled till at last, his money all was spent,
He told her they must leave their home, he could not pay the rent ;
She could not tell her father the sad and doleful tale,
So different from that happy time she left her native vale.

They went into cheap lodgings, and everything was sold ;
He enlisted for a soldier, and the rest soon may be told :
A friend and kindly neighbour for Gwendolin's father sent,
He came and brought her home, and in time grew quite content.

The music of the mill-wheel still is heard along the vale,
And many years have passed since the sad and doleful tale ;
One day a handsome soldier looked o'er the garden hedge :
They were happy ever after—he had signed the temperance pledge

WHAT IS LIFE ?

Oh ! what is life ? the cynic cries,—
   What do we live for here ?
But toil and moil, 'mid care and strife,
   Thro' every circling year ?
Our troubles start in early life
   With each hard puzzling task ;
We ponder over books when we
   In sunshine ought to bask.

And as in youth we drag along,
  Against the stream of life ;
Hoping a change will soon come round,
  We weary of the strife.
For stumbling blocks on every side,
  We meet from day to day ;
As we from youth to age advance,
  Plodding our weary way.

And when to manhood we are grown,
  Our cares still heavier press ;
We take unto ourselves a wife,
  Hoping to make them less.
But sad mistake : the burden grows ;
  And when we rise at morn,
We feel so much oppressed, we wish
  That we had not been born.

     ✺   ✺   ✳   ✳   ✳

Oh ! cynic, what a doleful strain,
  You croak into our ears ;
Have you no joy in life e'er found
  In all these many years ?
Did you in youth no happy hours,
  When tasks were over find ;
To cheer your heart with nature's joys,
  And elevate your mind.

Was it no sweet enjoyment then,
  To roam the fields and lanes ;
Or climb the glorious mountains high,
  When freed from lessons' chains ?

Did no response your youthful heart,
  In nature's gladness find ;
In joyous songs of happy birds,
  And healthful whispering wind ?

When hazel nuts in cops and brake,
  Hung thick on every bough ;
In gathering them was there no joy,
  For you to think of now ?
Where the pale starry primrose blooms,
  In dingle and in dell ;
Were you not drawn to their retreat,
  As by a magic spell ?

Thro' clover meadows spangled o'er,
  With cups of shining gold ;
Where bees hum gaily as they sip,
  The sweets that they enfold?
Was there no music in the streams,
  That murmur through the glades ;
Did you no sweet contentment find
  When resting in the shades?

Where timid hares and rabbits skip,
  And golden pheasants roam ;
And squirrels leap from bough to bough,
  To reach their lofty home ?
Are there no memories of that time,
  To wake a happy thought ?
If not, I say : you have not lived
  A life that each one ought.

When you a youthful maiden brought
  To share your gloomy home ;
Was selfishness the only cord,
  By which your heart was drawn ?

Was not the accents of her voice,
   Like music to your ears ;
And did not her sweet loving words,
   Dispel your gloomy fears ?

Of all created things man seems
   The only one to mourn,
Or heave a sigh of sad regret,
   That he was ever born.
The thrushes sing, the blackbirds pipe,
   The skylark warbles high ;
And tiny insects all rejoice :
   'Tis only man that sigh.

A bounteous hand supplies the earth
   With all his creatures need ;
If with enough they'd be content,
   Have less of selfish greed.
He gives us corn, and wine and oil,
   To feed and make us glad ;
Then wherefore, wherefore, cynic say :
   Why should your heart be sad ?

THE SNOWDROP.

THE snowdrop is peeping again from the earth,
We hail it with gladness, and welcome its birth ;
Sweet emblem of purity, first flower of spring,
Soon will all nature awaken and sing.
Soon will the crocus and daffodils tall,
Come forth at the sound of spring's gentle call ;
But the pale little snowdrop so pearly and white,
Comes e'er the winter hath taken its flight.

It comes bravely forth from the hard frosty ground,
To tell us that spring is soon coming round ;
With sweet feather'd minstrels to herald her way,
Singing more gaily each lengthening day.

The snowdrop is sought for with eager delight,
For the bridal at morn, and the ball room at night ;
The sick one's eye brightens, her face wears a smile,
In the pleasure the sweet buds afford her awhile.

No bird but the robin is heard yet to sing,
On the bare branch above that sweet pearly thing ;
He sits in the cold and pours forth his lay,
Bright, tuneful, and sweet as if it were May.

That sweet fragile flower, and pretty bright bird,
Teach all a lesson and make themselves heard ;
To shrink not in storms or cold winter's blast,
But cheerfully bear them, not long will they last.

A SONG OF PRAISE.
PSALM 104.

Praise the Lord my soul and spirit,
Glorious is His holy name ;
Clothed with majesty and honour,
Brighter than a living flame.
He the heavens like a curtain,
Spreadest with his mighty hand ;
Deck'st them out in gorgeous splendour,
Rich and beautiful and grand.

He commands the mighty waters,—
At His word they ebb and flow ;
Tho' they rage in fierce commotion,
Still no further can they go.

He hath set their bounds for ever,
Over which they cannot pass ;
Food he sends for all his creatures,
Wine and oil, green herb and grass.

Crystal streams flow to the rivers,
Sweet they meander through the hills ;
Giving drink for man and cattle,
And wild asses at their rills.
Song-birds make their home beside them,
In the branches sweetly sing
Praises to their great Creator,   .
Heaven's own high eternal King.

Wondrous are His works and mighty,
Sun and moon, and stars He rules ;
Changeless, silent in their courses,
Earth's foundation still he holds.
All creation now adore Him,
Sing His praise from shore to shore ;
And in worship bow before Him,
Singing, serving, evermore.

INGRATITUDE.

MEANEST of the human passions,
    Oh ! ingratitude art thou ;
Avarice and greed are pictured
    In deep furrows on thy brow.
All have trouble and misfortune ;
    Need a sympathizing friend ;
But if thou art hovering near them,
    Who a helping hand will lend ?

Even Charity so lovely,
    From thy presence soon will flee ;
And love, too, will no communion
    Long hold with a wretch like thee.
Friends and brothers thou hast parted,
    With thy grovelling, grasping greed ;
Sowing discord in their bosoms :
    Vile and poisonous is thy seed.

Oft destroying all the blossoms
    Springing in a generous breast,
With thy blighting scathing influence,
    Robbing it of peace and rest.
When a friend respected, trusted,
    Acts a base ignoble part—
'Tis the treachery unexpected,
    That strikes deepest to the heart.

A BRAW LAD IS JAMMIE.

A BRAW lad is Jammie, he says he lo'es me,
His twa' cheeks are rosy, sloe black is his e'e ;
But siller or gowd my Jammie has nane,
Sae the heart o' my father is hard as a stane.

He vows that my Jammie shall ne'er marry me,
And nane but a laird my husband must be ;
But I'll wed my Jammie, wi him gang awa,
In spite o'baith faither and mither, an mither an a'.

If Jammie's no siller he looks like a laird,
Can dance sae divinely, and sing like a bird ;
Na laird in the highlands like him is sa braw,
Sae I'll wed we Jammie in spite a them a'.

THE LOVELINESS OF NATURE.

Oh! lovely earth, I will sing thy praises,
 With heart and voice I will chant my lay;
Of glad green meadows and woodland mazes,
 Where joy-birds sing all the summer day.

And of the bright streams richly glowing,
 In life and beauty through all the land;
Refreshing the earth, and life bestowing,
 Sent for our use by a Father's hand.

Of country lanes, where white cots are peeping,
 From orchards rich with fruit-laden trees;
And cheerful voices of labourers reaping
 The golden corn waving in the breeze.

Of busy bees that return home laden,
 With sweets to store all their wondrous cells;
The soft sweet song of the blooming maiden,
 Mingling with the chimes of the evening bells.

Of the glorious sun in his radiant splendour,—
 Ruling the day; and the moon by night;
Of countless stars that unceasing render,
 Their gleaming beauty of glittering light.

Oh! wonderful world so full of lightness,
 My heart shall rejoice and thy praises sing;
But to Him who form'd all their glorious brightness,
 Still higher praise will my spirit bring.

POEMS FOR CHILDREN.

THE GOOD SHEPHERD.

PSALM XXIII.

GENTLE Shepherd, lead Thy children,
  Safe into the heavenly fold ;
And in verdant pastures feed them,
  Sheltered from the heat and cold.

When the streams of living waters,
  Ever flowing, sweetly glide ;
Teach them there renewing virtues,
  Be Thou ever at their side.

When alluring charms would lead them
  From Thy care to go astray ;
Guide the wanderer until safely
  Brought into the narrow way.

When temptations sore assail them,
  Gentle Shepherd, be Thou near :
When they tread the gloomy valley,
  With Thy staff support and cheer.

THE SONG OF THE FAIRY.

I'm a merry, merry fairy,
  My home's the sylvan shades;
I sleep away the sunshine,
  But in the moonlit glades
I dance to the music
  Of the spheres and the streams,
And revel with wood-nymphs,
  In their wild enchanting scenes.

CHORUS—
  I'm a merry, merry fairy,
    So happy, wild, and free ;
  And a merry, merry fairy,
    Forever I will be.

The nightingale sings sweetest
  When he knows I am there ;
The dewdrops are my jewels,
  With which I bind my hair.
I ring the pretty bluebells,
  To summon forth my maids ;
And bathe in crystal fountains,
  With the sportive water naiads.

The zephyrs are my chariots,
  They waft me far away :
When the early dawn is breaking,
  Before the glare of day.
I fly across the mountains,
  And sleep in rocky caves ;
A sunbeam for my pillow,
  My lullaby the waves.

THE PET THRUSH.

Published in the Children's Corner, "Preston Guardian."

I've got a pet thrush, with pretty brown wings,
He is such a pet, and oh ! how he sings ;
You all ought to hear him : talk of the lark,—
Why my thrush almost sings from daylight till dark.

He sits on his perch so fearless and bold,
In his white speckled vest, all shaded with gold ;
He bathes every morning to keep himself clean,
He's the bonniest birdie that ever was seen.

I call his name Bobby, and he knows it so well,
I love him much more than I ever can tell ;
He hops up and down on his perches so quick,
Like a clown or an harlequin playing a trick.

He's always so happy in his nice roomy cage,
And looks all around with the eye of a sage ;
Singing so gaily as he stands on one leg,
I think I can very soon teach him to beg.

But I must admit that his voice is yet low,
What can we expect in the cold frost and snow ;
When cold winter is past, and spring will appear,
His beautiful song will be heard far and near.

Sometimes I bring him a little fat worm,
This savoury morsel acts like a charm ;
When he's ate it all up, he whistles so loud,
As if he'd done something of which he was proud.

And woe to the fly that comes in his way,
No spider's fine parlour was ever so gay ;
Whenever one ventures inside Bobby's den,
He never is seen to come out again.

But some may think I am doing quite wrong,
In caging this bird for his sweet merry song ;
But Tabby had caught him, and hurt his poor wing,
I rescued him from her, the cruel old thing.

And now little dears, always bear this in mind,
If you wish to be happy, you must always be kind ;
Be kind to each other, be kind to the birds,
And they will repay you in songs without words.

COUNTRY SCENES AND PLEASURES.

Published in "The Preston Guardian."

Oh ! the bonny buttercups, with their golden sheen,
Glowing by the waysides, in meadow grass between ;
The bonny golden buttercups, what memories they bring
Of my happy childhood, when I gathered them in spring.

Oh ! the glorious woodlands, waving in the breeze,
Where primroses and violets bloom beneath the trees ;
And the bluebells springing from their mossy beds,
Sparkle with bright dewdrops, resting on their heads.

Oh ! the gushing cascade, in the ferny glen,
Sweet as angels' whispers, are its ripplings when
Its streams are gently falling o'er the mossy stones,
And roaring in wild fury when swollen by the rains.

Oh ! the happy song birds, warbling all the day,
Awaking sylvan echoes, with their joyous lay :
My memory often wanders back to those sweet hours,
When happy as the song birds, I roamed among their bowers.

Oh ! the shady dingles, where the purple bells,
Oft the stately foxglove, bend above the rills :
Where the squirrel, hare, and pheasant, make their quiet home,
And in sport and freedom, fearlessly can roam.

Oh ! the little lambkins, playing in the grass,
In their curly fleeces, bleating as you pass :
And the lowing cattle, wading in the streams,
All are glowing pictures, beautiful as dreams.

Oh ! the silver streamlets, shining in the sun,
Dancing o'er the pebbles, ever moving on ;
Rich in life and beauty, singing as they go,
Onward, ever onward, pure and sweet they flow.

Oh ! the mighty mountains, where the hart and roe,
Gambol in wild freedom, and sweet heath blossoms grow ;
Glorious in their grandeur, majesty, and might,
Where the lordly eagles, make their home at night.

Oh ! sweet are the pleasures of a country life,
Away from all the turmoil of city's noisy strife ;
They are pure and lasting, free as summer air,
And to all who love them, a joy for evermore.

THE LAW OF KINDNESS.

PUBLISHED IN "THE PRESTON GUARDIAN"

As a youth, named Harry Tomkins, was walking one day,
He saw a donkey carting a heavy load of hay ;
The burden it was heavy, but he pull'd his very best,
Till all at once he halted, as if he meant to rest.

The driver called out loudly, and flew in quite a rage,
As Harry stood by watching like a cynic or a sage ;
The driver pulled the bridle with all his might and main,
But Neddy turned out stupid, and would not start again.

He planted both his forefeet right firmly on the ground,
And all the driver's efforts could not make the wheels go round ;
He got a heavy cudgel, which he laid upon his back,
Till every blow he gave him was enough to make it crack.

But still the donkey stood there, he would not stir an inch,
And beneath those cruel blows he scarcely seemed to flinch ;
The driver turned to Tomkins, asked : did he ever see
A donkey half so stupid, as his knew how to be ?

You know not how to treat him, the youth to him replied,
I'll try if I can manage him, if you'll just stand aside ;
Let me see what I can do, I'm sure that's not the way,
To treat a poor dumb creature, as you have done to-day.

He went to cut some thistles that were growing near at hand,
And Neddy slily watched him,—he seemed to understand ;
He made a movement to him, and gave an eager sniff,
And soon with relish ate them, though they were a little stiff.

Then he stroked his shaggy mane, and spoke some kindly words,
And soon he felt the pleasure that a kindly act affords ;
For at once poor Neddy started as if he meant to trot,
And sheepish looked the driver at the lesson he had got.

THE BIRD'S NEST.

CHILDREN'S CORNER OF "THE PRESTON GUARDIAN."

WILLIE was in the garden, where grew apples, pears, and plums,
He went there very often to do his little sums ;
He thought he heard a twitter, not far from where he sat,
And at the place it came from he quickly threw his hat.

Up flew a tiny linnet, with a cry of fear and pain,
And Willie hastened to the spot from whence the linnet came ;
He found a nest so cosy, in it several little eggs,—
He went to tell his mother, fast flew his little legs.

He said, mother, may I have them ? they are such pretty ones,
I know a boy who's got some, and he's hung them up with strings.
Do, mother, come and get them, I'll show you where they are,
Just by that big old pear tree, in the hawthorn bushes there.

His mother said : my darling, I must do no such thing,
You quite forget the pain to the birdie that would bring ;
The little nest you speak of she made so snug and warm,
To rear her little young ones, and keep them safe from harm.

Each egg contains a birdie that in time will learn to sing,
And will give you far more pleasure than eggs upon a string ;
The happy little creatures were given to us in love,
Like the flowers, by Him who made them, to raise our thoughts
above.

We do not need the song-birds, nor yet the lovely flowers,
But they beautify and gladden this fair bright world of ours ;
So never ruthlessly destroy these gifts so kindly given,
But cherish them with loving care, as treasures sent from heaven.

BIRLEY WOOD.

PUBLISHED IN "THE PRESTON GUARDIAN," AUGUST 11TH, 1888.

ETHEL called out to her sister Mary,
　Oh do come out this bright and lovely day ;
And off she skipped, light as a little fairy,
　To chase the butterflies, as gay as they.

Mary was Ethel's elder sister,
　A sweet and gentle girl, thoughtful and good ;
She put on her hat and followed after,
　Together they set off to Birley Wood.

In and out they roamed among the mazes,
　Of that wild woodland—happy as the birds ;
And as they rested wove long chains of daisies,
　A pastime that to children delight affords.

Sweet wild roses bloomed upon the bushes,
　Their perfume floating on the summer air ;
And on the branches sang the merry thrushes,
　Their joyous songs resounding everywhere.

Little rabbits now and then came peeping,
　And nibbling the green herbage round about ;
Pheasants from the bushes too came creeping,
　But back they scar'd them with a merry shout.

The unseen cuckoo in a tree was calling,
　In oft repeated notes so clear and sweet ;
And water over mossy stones was falling,
　In rippling soothing murmurs near their seat.

They thought not of the time until the pealing
  Of evening chimes were wafted to their ears ;
O'er the meadows they came sweetly stealing,
  They knew then it was time for evening prayers.

At once they arose and lightly they bounded
  Through devious paths they quickly raced and ran ;
Their voices through the silent wood resounded,
  And woke the echoes fearful now to them.

They ran along, thoughtlessly unheeding
  The devious winding of the woodland ways ;
But they became so dense, they stopped, perceiving
  That they were in a strange bewildering maze.

They hastened back but could not find the turning
  That led into the path that passed their home ;
And with dismay they saw too, that the glooming
  And evening mists were quickly coming on.

Down Ethel's cheeks the tears began fast streaming,
  And to her sister in affright she clung ;
Wild and sad fancies through her mind were teeming,
  As shadows on their path grew dark and long.

Her sister said, remember, darling Ethel,
  Always to trust our heavenly Father's care ;
The Bible says that we need fear no evil,
  For He is with us always everywhere.

He feeds the little sparrows and the ravens,
  And clothes the beauteouslilies of the field :
Which of His tenderness and care are tokens
  That He will be to us a help and shield.

As Mary tried to cheer poor Ethel's sadness,
   They heard a dog bark in the wood quite near ;
Their hearts were filled at once with joy and gladness,
   And banished too was every anxious fear.

They called aloud, and the dog knew their voices,
   And bonn led through the brambles to their side ;
In wild delight he licked their hands and faces,
   In him they'd got a faithful trusty guide.

And as they stroked and fondly patted Rover,
   Their father came where they together stood ;
So all their troubles now were safely over,
   And Rover led the way from Birley Wood.

ONWARD.

Onward, onward, up and doing,
   Onward let your watchword be ;
But in honour all pursuing,
   From all pride and envy flee.
Let the truth guide all your actions,
   In your dealings all through life,
Tho' at times you may be weary,
   With the world's hard toil and strife.

When temptations strong beset you,
   When alluring charms would lead ;
Keep your heart and mind still steadfast,
   Guard your every word and deed.
Fools may scoff and sore deride you,
   Still let onward be your cry ;
If you find your courage failing,
   Call for aid to Him on high.

Tho' oft dim'd your spirit's brightness ;
  Tho' oft weary mind and limb ;
With the world's rebuffs you meet with,
  Keep your conscience pure within.
One hath said, in fiery trials
  I will bear you safely through ;
And when passing through deep waters,
  By your side I'll be there too.

TO THE BROOK.

Brooklet so busy, you toil night and day,
Through the green meadows you hasten away ;
Glowing in sunshine, singing you go,
Refreshing and sweet, your bright waters flow.

Where do you hasten to, sweet little brook,
You are always so lovely wherever we look ;
So bright and so merry, o'er the pebbles you skip,
Where whispering alders and willow trees dip.

Your pathway is ever through dingle and glade,
Where primroses bloom by your side in the shade ;
And tall foxgloves greet you, and nod as you pass,
Their beauty reflected as if in a glass.

And Jack Frost in winter your course cannot stay,
Though he places his crystals on each side your way ;
He has only just time to say—how do you do,
Before you are off, he's no power over you.

Does pleasure or duty prompt you to run,
Summer and winter, day and night like the sun ?
It must be duty and pleasure combined,
For flowers on your pathway you scatter behind

Go on little brooklet, you ever will be,
A thing of bright beauty and pleasure to me ;
I love your soft murmurs as sweetly you glide,
Refreshing the herb and the tree at your side.

THE BLACKBIRD'S SONG.

CHILDREN'S CORNER, "THE PRESTON GUARDIAN."

A BLACKBIRD was singing so sweetly,
  As he sat on a hawthorn spray ;
I heard the words he was singing,
  And this was his cheerful lay.
I love the beautiful sunshine,
  In freedom I fly through the air.
I can roam about in the woodlands,
  With never a sorrow or care.

I've a snug little nest in the bushes,
  For my mate and her children three ;
Jack, Dick, and Willie I call them :
  And for food they depend upon me.
But there is always abundance,
  Dispensed with a bounteous hand ;
I give thanks in songs of praises,
  For a banquet so rich and grand.

I dine off the choicest of dainties,
  Sweet flies with their gossamer wings :
Berries and fruit, ripe and tender,
  And all sorts of delicious things.

The richest of corn and barley,
    I get from the bright yellow sheaves ;
My table is laid out with flowers,
    And bright shining emerald leaves.

I drink of the clear crystal fountain,
    And bathe in the babbling brook ;
And when I take food to my children,
    My mate says how handsome I look.
And she is so blithe and so bonny,
    In her home with her little ones three ;
I wish all the world were as happy,
    As my dear little matie and me.

THE LORD'S PRAYER.

Hear my prayer, oh, heavenly Father,
Hallowed be Thy holy name ;
Thine the kingdom, where from glory,
Thy dear Son to earth once came.

Bend my spirit to submission,
Here on earth to do Thy will ;
And forgive each frail transgression,
Heavenly Father guard me still.

Give me strength that I may labour,
For the bread I daily need ;
And forgive me if I trespass,
From the way Thou would'st me lead.

Keep my heart and spirit upright,
Teach me to forgive a wrong ;
Give me strength to shun temptation,
As through life I walk along.

Thine the kingdom, Thine the glory,
Great eternal heavenly king :
Gracious Father hear and answer,
To Thy cross teach me to cling.

THE ORPHAN GIRL TO HER MOTHER IN HEAVEN.

You are gone, my mother, to a far brighter home.
And I'm left to mourn here, sad and alone :
In this cold world, full of sorrow and strife,
With no one to cheer the poor orphan girl's life.

But perhaps the kind Father, of which you've told me,
From His bright home above will my loneliness see ;
Oh, tell Him, dear mother, your child's left behind,
And perhaps a kind friend He for me may find.

I try not to mourn you : sad was your life here,
Many times have I seen the big silent tear
Fall from your eye, and I knew that you wept—
You thought that from me your trouble you'd kept.

They tell me, dear mother, you're a bright angel now,
With a harp in your hand, and a crown on your brow ;
Watch o'er me, mother, from your bright home above,
And guard me thro' life with a sweet angel's love.

A SONG FOR THE BAND OF HOPE.

Youths and maids of merry England,
  Come and join our band ;
Come and fight beneath our banner,
  In our cause so grand.

CHORUS.

Come and join us, come and join us,
  Come with heart and hand ;
Victory will crown the warfare,
  Of hope's glorious band.

Hope's the watchword on our banner,
  See it proudly waves ;
As the battle fiercely rages,
  With alcoholic slaves.

Their assaults are deep and deadly,
  Slaying thousands still ;
But we'll on to victory o'er them,
  And our vows fulfil.

Not with human foes our conflicts,
  They are spirits all ;
Come and join us, we will rout them,
  At our charge they'll fall.

EFFECTS OF DISOBEDIENCE.

A WEE little mousie was playing one day :
He began to feel hungry, and left off his play ;
He hunted all round for what he could find,
And soon smelt some cheese that was just to his mind.
He looked at the cheese, and he longed for a taste,
But some one was coming,—he ran back in haste.

Mousie told his mother about the nice cheese,
And said, may I fetch it now, mother, if you please ?
It's inside a box, with the door opened wide :
I can easily get it, if I go inside ;
And for our dinner it will be such a treat,—
I am so hungry, and want something to eat.

Oh no, my dear child, his mother replied :
Don't go in that box, or woe will betide,
For it is a trap, laid to catch such as you,
So keep away from it, whatever you do.
You did well to tell me,—I've seen them before,
And the cheese is to tempt you inside the door.

Not long after that, Mrs. Mouse fell asleep,
And mousie then thought he would like one more peep
At the savoury cheese,—there could be no harm,
And even the smell for him had a charm.
He was tempted inside,—it shut with a flap,
And poor little mousie was caught in the trap.

His mother awoke,—hearing the flap and a scream :
She thought she'd been having some horrible dream.
She ran to seek mousie, and found him at last :
The tears down his face were running quite fast ;
He looked so forlorn, and was in such a plight,
That she could not tell him : it just served him right.

But round to his prison she quietly stole,
And with her sharp teeth soon nibbled a hole.
Soon poor little mousie again was set free,
And promised nevermore disobedient to be.

MORAL.—

So when you are tempted, away from it run—
Or you will be caught as sure as a gun.

ENIGMA.

I ROAM through the meadows, in sunshine and shade,
I climb not the mountains, but in forest and glade ;
Silent, in solitude, alone, I am found,
Tho' I revel in freedom, in slavery I am bound.
In the midst of the sea, on the tempest I ride,
And like a great hero, my heart swells with pride ;
Without me the Queen would lose her degree,
Nor would an archbishop be appointed a see.
With the angels in heaven, I've always a place,
I begin every evil, and end in disgrace :
With demons in hades, in torments I lie,
And call out for mercy, who hears not my cry.
I was foremost in Eden, with man when he fell,
Both Eve and the serpent knew me quite well ;
My voice in debate is repeatedly heard,
In friendship and love, I'm true to my word.
Tho' always in trouble, I groan not nor sigh,
But never to be seen without a tear in my eye.
Now tell me my name, I'm sure you'll agree,
There's something mysterious and strange about me.

www.ingramcontent.com/pod-product-compliance
Lightning Source LLC
Chambersburg PA
CBHW032147010726
47493CB00008BA/2611